The Invisible Man

A play

Ken Hill

Incidental music by Brendan Healy

Based on the novel by H.G. Wells

Samuel French — London
New York - Toronto - Hollywood

ISBN 0 573 01793 X

Please see page vi for further copyright information

THE INVISIBLE MAN

First presented at the Theatre Royal, Stratford East, on 18th October, 1991. The cast was as follows:

Freda	Toni Palmer
The MC	Jonathon Whaley
Thomas Marvel	Brian Murphy
Millie	Liza Hayden
Dr Cuss	Miles Richardson
Mrs Hall	Toni Palmer
PC Jaffers	Geoffrey Freshwater
Teddy Henfrey	Jonathon Whaley
Miss Statchell	Caroline Loncq
Squire Burdock	Andrew Secombe
Wicksteed	Philip Newman
Griffin	Jon Finch
Fearenside	Miles Richardson
Reverend Bunting	Jonathon Whaley
Wadgers	Miles Richardson
Colonel Adye	Miles Richardson
Dr Kemp	Geoffrey Freshwater

Other parts by members of the company: Hayseed and Newsboy 2 by Miles Richardson; PC 1 by Andrew Secombe; PC 2, Newsboys 1 and 6 by Jonathon Whaley; PC 3 by Philip Newman; Newsboy 3 by Liza Hayden; Newsboy 4 by Geoffrey Freshwater; Newsboy 5 by Toni Palmer; Nurse by an ASM. Freda's Follies were Caroline Loncq, Liza Hayden, Miles Richardson, Andrew Secombe, Philip Newman and Geoffrey Freshwater. Miles Richardson also took part in ways not described in the text.

Directed by **Ken Hill**
Designed by **Robin Don**
Lighting Design by **Rory Dempster**
Illusions by **Paul Kieve**
Musical Direction and Keyboards by **Anthony Ingle**
Reeds by **Fran Reidy**
Percussion by **Eric Allen**

COPYRIGHT INFORMATION

(See also page ii)

Licences for amateur performances are issued subject to the understanding that it shall be made clear in all advertising matter that the audience will witness an amateur performance; that the names of the authors of the plays shall be included on all programmes; and that the integrity of the authors' work will be preserved.

The Royalty Fee is subject to contract and subject to variation at the sole discretion of Samuel French Ltd.

In Theatres or Halls seating Four Hundred or more the fee will be subject to negotiation.

In Territories Overseas the fee quoted above may not apply. A fee will be quoted on application to our local authorized agent, or if there is no such agent, on application to Samuel French Ltd, London.

VIDEO-RECORDING OF AMATEUR PRODUCTIONS

Please note that the copyright laws governing video-recording are extremely complex and that it should not be assumed that any play may be video-recorded for whatever purpose without first obtaining the permission of the appropriate agents. The fact that a play is published by Samuel French Ltd does not indicate that video rights are available or that Samuel French Ltd controls such rights.

Printed in Great Britain by Redwood Books Limited, Trowbridge, Wiltshire

The Invisible Man was then presented at the Vaudeville Theatre, London, on 6th February, 1993. The cast was as follows:

Freda	Toni Palmer
The MC	Jonathon Whaley
Thomas Marvel	Brian Murphy
Millie	Kerryann White
Dr Cuss	Miles Richardson
Mrs Hall	Toni Palmer
PC Jaffers	Larry Dann
Teddy Henfrey	Jonathon Whaley
Miss Statchell	Caroline Bliss
Squire Burdock	Andrew Secombe
Wicksteed	Philip Newman
Griffin	Michael N. Harbour
Fearenside	Miles Richardson
Reverend Bunting	Jonathon Whaley
Wadgers	Miles Richardson
Colonel Adye	Miles Richardson
Dr Kemp	Larry Dann

Other parts were played as before, except that Miss Statchell's understudy played the Nurse.

Understudies: Gary Lyons, John Halstead, Fiona Christie, and—internally—Miles Richardson and Jonathon Whaley.

Directed by **Ken Hill**
Designed by **Hayden Griffin**
Lighting Design by **Gerry Jenkinson**
Illusions by **Paul Kieve**
Incidental Music and Arrangements by **Brendan Healy**
Musical Direction and Keyboards by **Philip Dennis**
Second Keyboards by **Neil Drinkwater**
Percussion by **Mark Coldrick**

CHARACTERS

Freda
Follies
The MC
Thomas Marvel
Millie
Dr Cuss
Mrs Hall
PC Jaffers
Teddy Henfrey
Miss Statchell
Squire Burdock
Wicksteed
Griffin
Hayseed
Fearenside
Reverend Bunting
Wadgers
Colonel Adye
Dr Kemp
Newsboys
Policemen
Nurse

The action passes on the stage of the Empire Music Hall, Bromley

Time — 1904

PRODUCTION NOTE

In the original productions, there were two revolving three-sided towers (periaktoi) DR and DL, containing: the Wood Shed door, an interior door (adaptable to a cell door), and an arch, R; and the Pub door, an interior door (adaptable to a cell wall), and an arch, L.

Flown immediately upstage of these was a gauze, painted to represent exterior trees and foliage. Behind this was flown a cloth painted to represent an interior wall, which also acted as a blinder for the gauze.

Half-way upstage was flown a set of red curtains for the Village Hall, which had a banner attached, marked "Iping Village Defence Committee (Combating the Invisible Menace)"; and a cloth painted to represent the wall of the Cell and containing a barred window.

On a line further upstage, no UR and UL entrances being required, was flown a backing representing the rear wall of Kemp's Study. It contained a set of french windows.

The Pub interior was a truck which moved to a position allowing an entrance UR and UL. This was later adapted as the rear wall of Griffin's Room, utilizing the same two entrances.

On the same line, a backing that represented the Vicarage was flown in, which contained a sash-window and two niches for the busts.

Fully upstage was a cloth which represented the Village Green exterior, and which was also used as a backing for windows, doors, etc.

The wings consisted of three sets of revolving "flippers", one side painted to represent the Village Green exterior, the other all-purpose interior walls, which were dressed as necessary.

The floor was painted in a flagstone effect.

SYNOPSIS OF SCENES AND SET DESIGNS

ACT I

Scene 1 *How It All Began:* On the Stage
Gauze and blinder in; arches R and L

Scene 2 *The First Incident:* The Wood Shed. A late winter's night, earlier that year
Gauze and blinder in; wood shed R, Pub door L

Scene 3 *Arrival of a Mysterious Stranger:* The Saloon Bar. Same time
Blinder and gauze out; interior doors R and L; Pub unit UC, containing door C, windows either side; flippers R angled to permit entrance between Pub unit and second flipper; flippers L angled in similar fashion, dressed for bar backing; plain borders above; piano R, with stool; bar L with high stool; small round table C, with two stools; doormat; barrel to R of door; backing beyond

Scene 4 *The Strange Affair of the Dog:* The Village Green. A few days later
Gauze and blinder out; leafy borders in; Pub sign—"The Coach and Horses"—in; Village Green cloth in; wood shed door R. Pub door L; flippers R showing exterior scenes, straight on-off; flippers L showing Pub exterior, angled; entrances UR and UL; rustic table and chair R; village pump UC

Scene 5 *Burdock Has a Brain Wave:* A Country Lane. A little later
As Act I, Scene 1

Scene 6 *Robbery at the Vicarage:* The Vicarage. That night
Gauze and blinder out; plain borders; Vicarage flat upstage, containing sash window, lace and main curtains, niches either side for busts; Village Green cloth as backing;

interior doors R and L; flippers straight up and down both sides; pictures on both walls created R and L; entrances UR and UL; work table R, with one high and one low stool; harmonium L, with stool; carpet C

SCENE 7 *A Silly Conversation:* The Wood Shed. A few nights later
As Act I, Scene 2

SCENE 8 *Jaffers Makes an Arrest:* The Village Green. Same time
As Act I, Scene 4

SCENE 9 *Miss Statchell Takes Charge:* Outside Griffin's Room. Same time
Blinder in; arch R, interior door L

SCENE 10 *The Unveiling of the Stranger:* Griffin's Room. Same time
Gauze and blinder out; plain borders; Pub unit up stage adapted to Griffin's Room, containing recessed large window, covered in black cloth, black carpet. Village Green cloth as backing; interior doors R and L; flippers as Vicarage; no pictures; work table R with lab equipment; two stacked chairs downstage of it; tea-chest up stage of it; swivel chair UL; small table; boxes of chemicals; chair; full tea-chest L

ACT II

SCENE 1 *Setting the Scene:* On the Stage
As Act I, Scene 1

SCENE 2 *His First Disciple:* A Forest Glade. The following day
As Act I, Scene 1; log set by company R

SCENE 3 *Trouble at the Inn:* The Saloon Bar. A little later
As Act I, Scene 3

SCENE 4 *The Chase Begins:* A Country Lane. That night
As Act I, Scene 1

SCENE 5 *The Full Story:* Dr Kemp's Study. A little later
Gauze and blinder out; plain borders; Kemp flat UC, containing french windows; Village Green cloth as backing; interior doors R and L; flippers as Vicarage, but no entrances UR or UL; fireplace on wall R; picture on wall L; chair R; drinks table UR; screen UL; desk and chair L; carpet C

SCENE 6 *The Chase Continues:* Dr Kemp's Garden. Same time
As Act I, Scene 1

SCENE 7 *A Warning Is Delivered:* The Village Hall. A little later
Gauze and blinder out; red village hall curtains in; plain borders; banner in front of curtains; arches R and L; flippers turned for entrances R and L; "jumble sale" sign on flipper R; table C; 2 chairs R and L

SCENE 8 *The Reign of Terror:* Everywhere. The following week
Gauze in; arches R and L; plinth UC behind gauze

SCENE 9 *Plot and Counter-Plot:* The Police Station. One week later, noon
Gauze and blinder out; cell cloth in, containing small barred window; plain borders; cell door R; cell wall L; flippers straight up and down, closing off entrances; buckets on flipper R; bench with mattress UC; chair L

SCENE 10 *The Final Reckoning:* The Village Green. Same time
As Act I, Scene 4; later box and steps set behind gauze C

THE MUSIC

ACT I

Song 1 **1904!** Freda and the Follies

ACT II

Song 2 **Who's There?** Freda and the Follies

Song 3 **1904! (Reprise)** Company

The two songs "1904!" and "Who's There?" are available on hire from Samuel French Limited. The complete score of incidental music and musical effects (including the above songs) is available from:

LONDON MANAGEMENT
Noel House
2-4 Noel Street
London W1V 3RB

Telephone: 0171-287 9000
Fax: 0171-287 3236

THE ILLUSIONS

The illusions for the original production and subsequent tour and West End production of *The Invisible Man* were designed and built under the supervision of Paul Kieve. This Acting Edition carries descriptions of the effects of the illusions but does not attempt to describe the methods of achieving them. There are several reasons for this:

1. Many of the illusions as originally designed may well be too costly for some companies, particularly amateur groups.

2. The creation of the illusions required close collaboration between the designer, the lighting designer and the illusionist in order to conceal the technical back-up and devise customized props and furniture.

3. Some of the tricks involved are closely guarded secrets protected by the rules of the Magic Circle and these may not be published to the general public.

Any company contemplating a production of *The Invisible Man* is advised to employ if at all possible an illusionist or magic supervisor to help achieve the effects, most of which can be designed relatively simply. In the event that a prospective producer wishes to employ Paul Kieve's services in this context, application should be made to:

London Management
Noel House
2-4 Noel Street
London W1V 3RB

Telephone: 0171-287 9000
Fax: 0171-287 3236

ACT I

Scene 1

How It All Began

On the stage

The MC is mingling with the audience as it arrives

Long drum roll takes the House Lights out, ending on a cymbal clash as the MC bounds on stage in front of the Curtain, *lit by a follow spot*

MC (*waving his gavel*) Ladies and gentlemen, welcome to the Empire Music Hall on this mellifluous Monday (tumultuous Tuesday, wonderful Wednesday, thrilling Thursday, frenetic Friday, sensational Saturday) in the illustrious year of nineteen-o-four! (*He indicates*)

Music

The Curtain *rises*

Freda leads on the Follies from R

The MC retreats to watch from the steps, L

Song 1: 1904!

Freda (*singing*) Freda and her Follies are so pleased to ask you to
Salute another triumph for the old red, white and blue

Union Jacks flutter on R *and* L

Another flag is fluttering for us to stand and cheer
A year ago the Japanese, but now the French are here

French and Japanese flags are added R *and* L

New allies who have shaken hands and sworn a solemn oath

The Union Jacks disappear

That if the Kaiser wants to fight, he'll have to fight us both
We've got the men, we've got the guns, the ships we had before
So if we stand together, there can never be a war

All Nineteen-o-four!
That's the year we shall
Remember for the signing of the *entente cordiale*
Women We've sung the national anthem in a patriotic pose
Men We'd like to sing the *Marseillaise*...
Freda But we don't know how it goes

All Nineteen-o-four!
That's the year we shall
Remember for the signing of the *entente cordiale*
Men We'll fight with Corporal Camembert, we'll share a common trench
Women We'd like to wish him lots of luck...
Freda But no-one here speaks French

Group 1 Nineteen-o-four!
Group 2 Nineteen-o-four!
Group 3 Nineteen-o-four!
Freda Nine-
All -teen
Oh four!

The MC bounds back on stage, leading the applause

MC Thank you, Freda and the Follies! And now, let's have three rousing cheers for our new allies, the French and the Japanese!

The briefest of pauses

Thank you. (*He indicates Freda*) As most of you know, Freda is in real life that well-known actor-manager, Sir George Bluster——

Freda steps forward

As she speaks, her voice is doubled off by a recorded deep male voice

Freda Evening.
MC —and the Follies, his troupe of classically-trained actors and actresses——

Freda turns upstage to present them, and they all preen

—all masters of disguise——

Drum beat. The men snatch off their moustaches. The women applaud

—who can play many and varied roles——

The Follies go into roles: 1 as Isobel in East Lynne*—"Dead, dead, and never called me mother"; 2 as Little Nell—"Spare a copper for a poor waif, guv'nor"; 3 as Richard III—"A horse, a horse, my kingdom for a horse"; 4 as Quasimodo—"The bells, the bells"; 5 as Long John Silver—"Ah, Jim, lad"; 6 as Polonius in* Hamlet*—"And borrowing dulls the edge of husbandry"; Freda as Dick Whittington—"Five more miles to London, Dick, and not a puss in sight"*

The MC cuts them off, but 6 keeps going—"Unto thine own self be true" and has to be cut off again by the MC

—and who will shortly be using this skill and versatility while acting out their differing roles for you during the remainder of this evening's entertainment. So let's ask them to hurry into their new costumes and characters, and return to us in just a moment or two, three, four!

Play-off

The Follies dance off, R

Yes, ladies and gentlemen, just a moment or two, and it will be time for our main event, which tonight takes the form of a chilling dramatic presentation entitled——

Cymbal

"The Terrible Tale of the Awful Events at the Village of Iping!"

Drone. Lighting checks, turns green

Ladies and gentlemen, a unique piece of fantastic theatre is on offer tonight, for not only does it star the famous Follies, not only is it based upon certain recent true events, but—and at *enormous expense* to the owners here at the Empire Music Hall—it is presented for you personally by a man whose actual participation in the dreadful doings has made him a household name. A big warm round of applause, then, for the only living survivor prepared to stand up and tell his tale—that reprobatious rapscallion ragamuffin—Mr Thomas Marvel!

Fanfare

Marvel enters R, *lit by a follow spot. He sports a frock coat and waistcoat over his character clothes, and raises his top hat*

The MC moves down the steps a little, L, *as Marvel moves to* C, *clowning. The towers turn to pub and wood shed*

Marvel (*to the audience*) Thank you for that wonderful sitting ovation. (*To the MC*) And thank *you*, sir, for that splendid introduction. I must say you're looking remarkably handsome this evening. Must be the drink.

MC (*indignantly*) I haven't had a drink!

Marvel No, but I have. (*To the audience*) Well, now you know what you're in for, you may as well leave. No, no, I jest. Sit, madam. What we can do is to *begin the story*. So here goes. (*He declaims*) I—Thomas Marvel—a Gentleman of the Road——

MC (*still smarting*) A tramp.

Marvel (*to him*) I'll call myself what I like, and don't interrupt. The owners of this theatre are paying me a guinea a night to recount the 'ideous 'appenings at Iping, and these people want to hear me doing so, and enjoy themselves. Don't you, madam? Am I right, sir? Of course I am. We all love a bit of cruelty. They want to hear the dreadful screams. They want to smell the dripping blood. They want to taste the fear as the 'orrible events unfold before their very eyes.

MC (*wearily*) They also want you to get on with it.

Marvel Then I shall. On with the motley, my good man. *Sed fugit interea, fugit tempus.*

MC What does that mean?

Marvel Piss off.

MC Right! That does it! (*He storms into the auditorium*) I'm getting the Manager!

Marvel Get me one, as well, will you. A short fat one with hairy legs.

MC (*disappearing; shouting off*) And you—fetch me a pint of porter!

He exits

Marvel (*to the audience*) I'm sorry about that, ladies and gentlemen. They're all the same, these MCs. They think they run the show.

Pause

Well, you might as well laugh—you won't get your money back. (*To the Musical Director*) Mood, maestro, please. Time to tell the story.

Drone. Lighting checks, goes green again

It all happened earlier this year—the third anniversary of the death of the old Queen. Do you remember her, madam? The old Queen? Oh, you do! Then you'll remember that terrible winter, one of the worst in living memory.

Projected snow falls, and a cold wind blows. Xylophone

I myself hadn't yet appeared on the scene—but somebody else was about to—if "appearance" is the right word—in the Saloon Bar of the only pub in the Village of Iping—— (*He indicates the pub* L)

A (recorded) tinny pub piano is heard through the wind

—though it really began a bit earlier (*He indicates the wood shed door* R)—round the back—by the wood shed.

He disappears into the auditorium, R, *where he remains, watching, changing into his full "character" clothes. As he does so, the door* L *opens, spilling out light*

Scene 2

The First Incident

The Wood Shed

A late winter's night. Earlier that year

Millie appears, L, *wearing a shawl*

Millie (*calling behind her*) It's cold, Mrs Hall!
Mrs Hall (*off*) Why d'you think we need the firewood, you silly tart? Now get on with it!

Millie hurries to the shed, lifts the latch, then turns back suddenly. A sinister drone

Millie (*peering about*) Is there anybody there?

She sees nothing, and goes into the shed, leaving the door open, on the back of which hangs a bright silvery saucepan

Dr Cuss enters from the pub, carrying his bag, wearing black coat and hat, a shiny badge on one lapel

The drone ends on a thin high sting. Dr Cuss crosses R

Millie reappears, carrying wood, and nearly bumps into him

Oh, Dr Cuss! You didn't half make me start!
Dr Cuss You always had good reflexes, Millie.

He fondles her

High time we tested them again, eh?
Millie (*not meaning it*) I'll scream for help.
Dr Cuss I don't *need* any help. (*He releases her*) I'll wait in the wood shed.
Millie Mrs Hall'll be watching me.
Dr Cuss I'm in no hurry.

Millie Honestly! And you a JP, an' all!

Giggling, she goes into the pub, closing the door behind her

Dr Cuss Stupid girl. She's only fit for this. (*He goes to enter the shed, pauses, turns back quickly*)

A sting and drone

Someone here?

He sees nothing, goes into the wood shed, and closes the door

The drone continues, then three chords ascend. After the third, the latch on the door lifts, and the door swings open

(*Off*) That was quick.

The saucepan twitches, then is lifted off its nail

(*Off*) Millie? Is that you, Millie? Millie? Millie?

The saucepan goes quickly into the shed. A loud clonk, and a cry from Dr Cuss

Black-out

Scene-change music. During the Black-out, the door closes, the two towers revolve to interior doors, the blinder flies out, and Light bleeds through the gauze to:

Scene 3

Arrival of a Mysterious Stranger

The Saloon Bar. Same time

Mrs Hall is behind the bar, Jaffers seated on a high stool at the bar, Teddy at the piano, Millie UR, *having dropped a piece of wood on the floor. All are with heads up, listening. The gauze flies out and Light fills from the front*

Mrs Hall D'you hear that? Sounded like a scream.
Jaffers Only the wind, Mrs Hall. Fill her up again, there's a pet.

Teddy plays, Millie picks up her piece of wood

Mrs Hall (*pulling*) I'll be glad when this cold spell's over. It's murdering my chilblains.
Millie (*moving* UL) It'll be spring soon—don't you think, Mr Jaffers?
Teddy Policemen don't think, Millie. They've been trained to discipline. (*He heaves with silent laughter*)
Mrs Hall No sarcasm, if you please, Teddy Henfrey. It belittles the mind, and in your case that's a dangerous thing to do.
Jaffers No lady in his life, Mrs Hall. Makes a man hard.

He pats her hand

I've mentioned this before.
Mrs Hall (*pulling her hand away*) Mention marriage, and I might pay attention.

A gust of wind, a swirl of snowflakes and Miss Statchell enters purposefully, UC

Miss Statchell Good-evening, everybody.

Teddy stops playing. All stare at Miss Statchell, as she puts her bag down on a barrel to the right of the door, and begins taking off her coat

Mrs Hall Miss Statchell, I've told you before. We don't serve unaccompanied ladies in here.
Miss Statchell You said I was no lady for coming *in* unaccompanied.
Mrs Hall No more, you ain't.
Miss Statchell Then you may serve me. You'll have my requirements in a while. (*She shakes snow over Teddy*) Sorry about that. Some fool outside nearly ran me over. (*She takes her coat off* UR) I think he was drunk.

She exits

A gust of wind, swirl of snowflakes, and Burdock—swathed in a leather coat, flying helmet, gauntlet, goggles—enters, UC, *followed by Wicksteed*

Burdock Evening, everybody !

General greetings. Teddy resumes playing

All Evening, Squire—Mr Wicksteed.

Wicksteed assists Burdock off with the coat

Wicksteed Allow me, Squire.
Burdock Thank you, Wicksteed. (*To the others*) What a filthy night.
Teddy Ay, Squire. It's all this bad weather.
Burdock Yes.

Millie enters

(*Turning*) Hallo, Millie! How's the bicycle?
Millie (*puzzled*) I haven't got a bicycle, sir.
Burdock Really? That's odd. Could have sworn somebody told me you were the village——
Wicksteed (*coughing quickly*) I'll get you a port, sir. (*He takes the coat* UR)
Burdock Yes, make it a port, would you? (*To the others*) Good chap, Wicksteed. Obeys orders before they're given.

Wicksteed crosses below him to the bar, where he orders the Squire's port during the following

Mrs Hall Servants are supposed to think quicker than you, Squire—and just as well.
Burdock You're right, there.

Miss Statchell enters

If Wicksteed hadn't grabbed the brake just now, we'd have run over some silly screaming female.

Miss Statchell overhears this

I think she was drunk. (*He turns to find himself facing her*)

A brief pause

(*To her*) Can I get you a drink?
Miss Statchell A large Glen McCraggie, please.

She crosses down to the stool right of the table, and sits

Burdock Right! One large Glen McCraggie coming up. (*He crosses to Wicksteed; lowers his voice*) Wicksteed, what the hell's a Glen McCraggie?
Wicksteed A rather earthy malt from the Isle of Mull, sir. (*To Mrs Hall*) Put some nutmeg in that Empire Made Whiskey. She won't spot the difference. (*To Burdock*) I used to be a barman in Bangkok.

Teddy's piano-playing slows as he leers at Miss Statchell, but one glare from her and he resumes

Burdock (*regarding Miss Statchell*) But who is she?
Wicksteed (*handing him his port*) The new schoolmistress, sir. You approved the appointment yourself.
Burdock I did? How astute of me. (*He goes to Miss Statchell*)

Millie sneaks the door open to attempt her assignation

Mrs Hall (*as Burdock goes*) I preferred the old one. Ga-ga, but God-fearing. (*To Millie*) Millie! What d'you think you're doing?

Millie closes the door quickly, and polishes the window with a duster. Teddy jumps and stops playing

Millie I'm cleaning the windows, Mrs Hall.
Mrs Hall Well, don't. Them dusters cost money.

During the following, Millie goes to flirt with Teddy, while Mrs Hall prepares Miss Statchell's "Glen McCraggie". Burdock beams on Miss Statchell, indicating the stool, L: *"May I?" and sits down*

Burdock Sorry about the car just now. (*He holds out his hand*) The name's Burdock, by the way—Squire Burdock—but my chums all call me Bonzo.

Miss Statchell Try hitting them.

Burdock (*amused by this sally*) Very good. You're from Edinburgh, aren't you?

Miss Statchell Glasgow. But I'll give you one mark for getting the country right.

She puts a pipe in her mouth, and prepares to light it

Burdock (*a little taken aback*) And what brings you to our little neck of the woods?

Miss Statchell I was arrested as a suffragette in Paisley Road, and put in Duke Street Prison. After that, your miserable little village was the only job I could get. But you'll know all that from my application.

Behind them Wicksteed sniffs the "Glen McCraggie" and makes a face

Burdock Oh, I never read those things. They're all about your education, intelligence, stuff like that. Never anything useful in them.

Wicksteed Your Glen McCraggie, miss.

He places it down and backs off to watch

Burdock All this harping on knowledge. Take the other day.

Miss Statchell sniffs her "Glen McCraggie", gives Wicksteed a look. He retreats to the top end of the bar. Miss Statchell takes a flask out of her bag

Jumped a very small horse over a very large ditch. Everybody said afterwards that it couldn't be done. Well, if I'd *known* that I wouldn't have done it, would I? Pretty useless stuff, knowledge, I find. Give me ignorance any day. You know where you are if you don't, if you catch my drift.

Miss Statchell Oh, yes. (*She pours her drink into his and tops her glass up from her flask*) You're an unusual man, Squire Burdock. Self-awareness is rare in morons.

Burdock (*staring at his glass*) Isn't that the truth?

Loud gust of wind, big swirl of snow, and Griffin enters. Griffin wears Dr Cuss's clothes, carries his doctor's bag. Every inch of him is covered, his face bandaged, dark goggles over his eyes

Big sting of music, and sinister drone underlay. All react back, Burdock to bar L, *Miss Statchell to below piano* R

A pause

Griffin (*in a low harsh voice; to Mrs Hall*) Are you the innkeeper, madam?
Mrs Hall And if I am?
Griffin I'd like a room. (*After a pause*) This is an inn. Inns have rooms.
Mrs Hall Millie, take the gentleman's bag.

Millie steps forward. Griffin turns on her. Sting in the underlay. She reacts back with a cry. Mrs Hall comes round the bar

Oh, give it here, you daft cat. I'll do it myself.

Griffin turns on her. Sting in the underlay. She gingerly takes the bag

If you'd care to come this way, sir.

She leads the way off DL, *followed by Griffin, the music moving with him*

He turns back in the doorway. Sting, and all find somewhere else to look. He sees Miss Statchell, and—for a moment—is still, the music softening

Then he goes, closing the door, and the drone stops

Jaffers (*crossing* UC, *awe-struck, looking off after him*) Peculiar-looking beggar, ain't he?
Teddy (*joining him,* R) Accident, I suppose.

Burdock and Wicksteed join the group, L. *Millie moves* DR

Miss Statchell (*joining him,* R) To his whole face?
Wicksteed Could be a war wound, miss. I used to be a White Missionary in ninety-three, and the Matebele did some very nasty things.

Burdock The ladies don't wish to know that, Wicksteed.

Wicksteed No, sir.

Burdock Besides, even those blighters leave a fellow's face on. This chap's been completely wiped out. He's lacking the whole kit-and-caboodle.

Miss Statchell (*picking up her pipe*) I once toured a sweat-shop owned by an English lord where they were using lead glaze. That wasna very pretty.

Jaffers I'm sure he complied with the by-laws, miss, if he was of the gentry.

A hand appears at the top edge of the door behind them, although its owner is masked by the tight group, UC

Anyway, it's your hands that fall off with that stuff.

Millie can see the hand, and points at it, making gurgling noises. All stare at her, turn to look, yell, and react R *and* L, *revealing Dr Cuss hanging on the door, his back to us, totally nude*

Millie (*recognizing him immediately*) It's Dr Cuss !

He collapses. She runs to the table to stare at him, then faces to the front

And not a stitch on him!

Black-out, scene-change music, the gauze and blinder fly in. The Light builds on:

Scene 4

The Strange Affair of the Dog

The Village Green. A few days later

Marvel ascends the stage, R, *now fully dressed in his tramp's character clothes, carrying a bundle on a stick over his shoulder*

Marvel (*to the audience*) *That* got you going, didn't it, madam? I'll bet you thought I was the only bum in the show. It also got Dr Cuss going, as he had no choice now but to leave the village, vowing vengeance on the villain who had attacked him and stolen his clothes—assumed to have been a jealous husband or a patient with a grudge—and he had a lot of *them.* It also took the curtain up on that strange and terrible year in which the arrival of the mysterious stranger was but a prelude to a sequence of more mystery, and even tragedy. As for me, I was enjoying my usual idyllic itinerant existence; that's walking about, madam—doing nothing—when one of those curious circumstances of chance you wish had never happened conspired to bring *me* to the village. Yes, ladies and gentlemen—Thomas Marvel—gentleman of the road—acclaimed world expert at doing sod-all—found himself within the peaceful tranquillity of the little village of Iping.

Village music. Towers turn to wood shed R, *pub door* L, *the blinder flies out, and Light bleeds through the gauze to reveal a village scene—Mrs Hall doing the washing on a tub on the table,* R; *the Hayseed carrying a pitchfork* RC; *Jaffers on his bicycle* C; *Teddy humping a milk churn* ULC; *Millie sitting on a stool, and peeling potatoes into a bucket* DL. *All are facing front, frozen, with fixed smiles. Marvel indicates the pub*

Here—believe it or not—outside the very pub in which the mysterious stranger had set up his lodgings—(*he indicates a window above*)—up there creating consternation in the household with his bizarre appearance—and where simple country folk went about their daily pursuits…

All come to life: the gauze flies out, Light fills the stage from the front

Jaffers wheels his bike off UR

Teddy carries the churn into the wood shed, and returns with a barrel which he carries off UL

The Hayseed accosts Marvel

Hayseed (*to Marvel*) Ah.
Marvel Ah.
Hayseed (*indicating the sky*) Ah.
Marvel (*agreeing*) Ah.
Hayseed (*indicating the pub*) Ah?

Marvel (*shaking his head*) Ah.
Hayseed Oh, ah!
Marvel Oh, ah!

The Hayseed goes into the pub, and the music stops

Marvel (*to the audience*) What the hell was all that about? (*He resumes his narration*) ...and where I was greeted in a typically English village manner.
Mrs Hall (*to Marvel*) And who are you when you're at home, you horrible little hobgoblin?
Marvel (*putting down his bundle and taking out his spoons*) Thomas Marvel at your service, ma'am. Marvel by name, and marvellous by nature—(*to the Musical Director*) two, three...!

Music: a jig. He plays the spoons

Mrs Hall Oy!

The spoons fly in the air to hit the cloth. Marvel gathers them up

What d'you think you're doing?
Marvel I'm singing for me supper.
Mrs Hall No wonder you're so thin. You want food, you'll have to earn it. Get out back, and chop some wood.
Marvel (*scandalized*) *Work* for a living? The Brotherhood of the Road would strip me of me stick and bundle!
Mrs Hall I'll strip you of your head, in a minute. Now hop it.
Marvel Round the back, you say? (*To the audience*) Patience, madam. I shall return.

A jig

He dances off, UL

Teddy enters, carrying a barrel, to look off after him, then smiles on Millie

Mrs Hall Silly bugger. Just 'cos I got a soft heart. (*To Teddy*) Don't stand there like a dying duck! Get on with it!

Teddy scoots off into the wood shed DR, *never to return*

Miss Statchell enters briskly UR, *crossing to Millie*

Miss Statchell (*brightly*) Good-morning, Millie! (*Less brightly*) Good-morning, Mrs Hall.
Mrs Hall And what can we do for you *this* time?
Miss Statchell I was hoping Squire Burdock might be here.
Mrs Hall Well, he ain't. Nobody's here.
Millie Not even the new lodger with the bandaged head.
Mrs Hall Him? He's *never* here. And when he is, you don't know where he's come from. He's either outside having not gone out, or he's inside having not come in.
Miss Statchell Is that a fact?
Millie It's really mysterious.
Mrs Hall Like your head. Now get them spuds on, or I shall have to cancel this month's night off.
Millie Oh no, Mrs Hall!

Wailing, she runs into the pub, with the bucket

Miss Statchell A potent threat, it appears.
Mrs Hall All she does is walk five miles to the nearest town and buys a Penny Dreadful. (*She crosses to her, with the tub*) But it's the high spot of her pathetic existence, so I hold it over her head like the Sword of Damocales (*sic*). (*She crosses to the pub*) Now if you don't mind, *some* of us have got work to do.

She goes into the pub

Miss Statchell crosses to the table, perches on it, takes out a notebook and begins to write in it. A brief pause

A sinister drone as Griffin appears UL, *smoking*

A pause. She becomes aware of his presence, turns, and rises. He lifts his hat

Griffin You're new here.
Miss Statchell Aren't we both?

Griffin (*with grim amusement*) Oh, I'm new all right. There's never been anybody like *me* before. (*He moves downstage*)

The music is softer

We must get to know one another better.
Miss Statchell I'll look forward to it.

Music stops

Mrs Hall and Millie enter

Mrs Hall Oh, so *you've* shown yourself, have you? And where were *you* at breakfast?
Griffin (*furiously*) I've told you I don't eat in front of people!
Mrs Hall And I've told you I don't serve in the rooms. I've got too much to do.

He turns on her. Big sting

Griffin I'm expecting some luggage to be delivered from the station.
Mrs Hall I don't carry bags up, neither.
Griffin (*moving close*) What *do* you do, Mrs Hall?
Mrs Hall (*just holding her ground*) As little as possible, same as the rest of us.
Griffin In my rooms, Mrs Hall. Soon as it arrives.

Brief pause

Mrs Hall Yes, sir.

Griffin goes into the pub, taking off his hat

The drone stops. Mrs Hall finds Millie grinning at her

And *you*! Wipe that gormless grin off your face, and get that back inside! (*She indicates the stool, and turns upstage, in time to meet:*)

Burdock and Wicksteed, who enter UR. *Burdock sports a natty button-hole. Millie flies off into the pub*

I'm not running a clinic for the incurably idle.

Burdock Ah, the jovial Mrs Hall, our jolly publican! Isn't it a lovely day? (*He sniffs the buttonhole*) Spring's in the air, what?

Mrs Hall If you like. Me, I'm off to smash the ice on the water-butt.

She exits UL

Burdock turns on Miss Statchell, affecting extreme surprise. Wicksteed crosses UL *to look off after Mrs Hall, the three of them forming a diagonal*

Burdock And Miss Statchell, too! What an unexpected pleasure!

Miss Statchell For *you*, perhaps. (*To Wicksteed. Sweetly*) Good-morning, Mr Wicksteed.

Wicksteed (*raising his hat*) Good-morning, miss. I told the Squire I'd seen you heading in this direction.

Miss Statchell Did you now?

Wicksteed Yes. We were just coming——

Burdock (*irritated*) Thank you, Wicksteed, that'll do. We were coming here, anyway. (*To her*) Did you receive my card?

Miss Statchell The one with a gold rim and gothic letters, inviting me to Burdock Hall for dinner? I could hardly miss it, Squire.

Burdock Then when shall we have you?

Miss Statchell Never, is my guess. The schoolhouse is dilapidated, the accommodation provided isn't fit for human habitation, and this—(*she hands him a torn page from her notebook*)—is my resignation.

Burdock (*open-mouthed, staring at it*) There's nothing I can do to make you change your tune?

Miss Statchell Not unless you've taken a course in Mind Control. Now if I could just——

Yapping of a dog, and Fearenside enters UR, *pulling a laden cart, a small dog nodding over one corner*

Fearenside Mind your backs! Coming through!

Burdock Oh, morning, Fearenside.

Fearenside Morning, Squire. (*He drops the cart* C, *crossing to its left to call up*) Delivery from the station! (*He sees the dog taking an interest*) Get down, Mafeking, you little swine.

The dog slinks down out of sight

(*To Miss Statchell*) Morning, miss. Settling in, are we?

Miss Statchell Not so far. (*To Burdock*) Now if I could just——

Mrs Hall enters from UL

Millie enters from the pub

Mrs Hall Oh, Jim, am I glad *you're* here. That queer-ball upstairs has been going on about his stuff summat alarming. "Is it here? Is it here? Why isn't it here?" What is it, anyway?

Fearenside Ah, funny stuff. (*He takes the top off the box to reveal rows of bottles*) Looks like chemicals.

Ping. All look to the front

Miss Statchell (*recovering*) Really? I know something about those. (*She goes to the head of the cart*) We'd better take a look. They can be hazardous.

Mrs Hall (*protesting feebly, burning with curiosity*) It is private property, you know.

Miss Statchell We have a right to inspect for dangerous substances, Mrs Hall. It's a free country—occasionally.

By now, they are all poking about in the cart, Mrs Hall lifting out a large jar. She moves DL *a little, Burdock and Wicksteed move to Miss Statchell's right, Fearenside and Millie to her left. The dog lifts up its head again*

Burdock All the same, not very pukka, poking about in a chap's personal kit… (*He brings out a paper*) Hallo. Here's something *very* unusual.

Wicksteed What's that, sir?

Burdock A polite letter from a bank.

Wicksteed expresses amazement, returns to the cart as Burdock breaks R *a little, reading it*

He's withdrawn all his funds.

Miss Statchell (*holding up the bottles*) Queer selection, I must say. This one's lead monoxide, but this green one's got me baffled.

Wicksteed takes it from her

Wicksteed I think you'll find it's arsenic trioxide, miss. Quite distinctive, and rather interesting.

Burdock How so?

Wicksteed Well, I used to be apprentice to a Venetian glass-blower, and these compounds are used in its manufacture—one as a decolourizer, the other to produce crystals of a particularly high transparency.

Burdock (*thoughtfully*) So. You think he's a glass-blower?

Mrs Hall Oh, well, that would account for it. Him having no face.

As they stare

I mean, if one day he sucked instead of blowed.

Wicksteed (*after a brief pause, rescuing the others from embarrassment*) Molten glass is certainly very dangerous. However...

They return to the cart, poking and prodding in ad-lib

Griffin comes out of the pub and sees them. Sinister drone. He crosses to R

Griffin *What are you doing*?

Big sting. All react back guiltily. Griffin goes to the cart, touching his belongings

Who told you to touch my things? How dare you!

The dog grabs his sleeve growling. Griffin struggles to free himself

Fearenside (*to the dog*) Get down, you little tyke! Go on, get down, there!

Griffin finally pulls free, but in the process knocks off his glasses. There are two black holes where his eyes should be. He takes two staggering steps forward, each marked by a high thin sting, then claps a hand over them

Griffin My glasses... (*He kneels, searches for them blindly, one hand still over the eye-holes*) Help me...

Fearenside, DL, *takes a step forward, but lacks the courage, and backs off again*

For God's sake, can't anybody see I need some help!

Miss Statchell moves forward, finds the glasses, kneels to his right, presses them into his hand, the music softening

Miss Statchell Here.
Griffin Thank you. (*He puts them back on, holds them in place, and looks searchingly at her*) You're not frightened of me. That's good.

She rises

(*To the others*) My eyes… There was an accident.

He hurries into the pub, shutting the door behind him

The music stops. Fearenside stands by the pub door, looking off after him. Mrs Hall moves down to Fearenside

Mrs Hall (*to Fearenside*) That dog of yours ought to be in the river with a brick.

Its head appears, and she turns on it

(*To the dog*) Oh yes, you should.

It sinks down out of sight again

(*To Fearenside*) What's up?
Fearenside Him—he's *black*.
Burdock What are you talking about, man?
Fearenside I seen inside his sleeve where it were ripped. It were just *black*—like coal.
Millie (*crossing to the head of the cart*) That must be why he's wearing the bandages! He's trying to hide the colour of his skin.
Miss Statchell Silly girl. Why would anybody do such a thing?
Wicksteed To disguise himself, miss. Which means, of course, that he may be a criminal.

All react, then thoughtfully move to different parts of the Green, to think

Mrs Hall (*looking up at the window, moving* UL) In my rented rooms?

Wicksteed On the run, you see.

Millie (*crossing to above the table*) Hiding his face so he can't be recognized.

Fearenside (*crossing* R) Telling everybody round here it were an accident.

Burdock (*coming down right of the cart*) Very convincingly, too. Must have been a major crime.

Miss Statchell passes him, crossing to upstage left of the cart

Wicksteed (*coming down left of the cart*) Could be this anarchist they're looking for, sir—the one who garrotted the Home Secretary. Our mystery man fits the description.

Burdock (*looking up at the window*) Wicksteed, our man hasn't *got* a description.

The dog lifts its head to observe the following. Mrs Hall moves down to behind Wicksteed

Wicksteed No, sir, but he never takes his gloves off, and they're looking for a dark-skinned man with a tattoo on the back of his left hand.

Mrs Hall (*in his ear, making him jump*) Well, *I'll* have his gloves off him!

The dog disappears, and Mrs Hall crosses R

No criminal villain's hiding out on *my* licensed premises.

Miss Statchell (*coming down left of the cart, left of Wicksteed*) This is pure speculation. The man may be exactly what he claims to be—the victim of a serious accident.

Mrs Hall Then he can *prove* it to us, can't he?

All fall silent as Griffin reappears from the pub—a little tentative, this time

Griffin Mrs Hall, I really do need my things inside. (*He crosses to* C) I'm sorry about earlier. I'm... Still in pain... From the accident.

They don't react

(*His anger returns*) Well? Have I got to stay out here all day? Or do you want to search *me*, too?

Fearenside (*moving in a little*) Well, I wouldn't mind having a look at that hand my dog bit.

Griffin (*putting his hand in his pocket*) Why?

Fearenside I'm responsible. Let's have a look.

Griffin It's not necessary.

Mrs Hall Have you got something to hide?

Burdock (*moving in*) I'm afraid we may have to insist, old chap.

He takes Griffin's left arm

Griffin What is all this?

Burdock Wicksteed.

Wicksteed takes the other arm

Griffin Are you people mad?

Fearenside moves in to pull off the glove. They struggle round in a half-circle

No! No!

Fearenside pulls the glove off, breaking L *in his reaction to what he sees. Burdock and Wicksteed react* R, *to Mrs Hall. Griffin stands still,* RC, *holding his arm out rigidly towards Fearenside. He has no hand. Big sting of music, and continuing. Fearenside throws the glove down. Griffin holds the pose, then turns* R

Are you satisfied? Seen enough? (*He turns in a circle, holding the handless sleeve out at them*) Go on—have a good look! (*He reaches out towards Fearenside*)

During the following, Fearenside jerks back, turns upstage, moving slowly around to the head of the cart, his back to us. Griffin kneels to pick up his glove. The music stops. Burdock moves forward, very embarrassed

Burdock Awfully sorry, old chap. We thought it was just the—(*he*

indicates his face) We didn't realize you were also short of a—(*he indicates his hand*) We were——

Miss Statchell (*rescuing him*) They were very concerned about these chemicals of yours.

Griffin (*rising*) Then they've no need to be. They're part of my work, and they're quite harmless.

Miss Statchell Even arsenic trioxide?

Griffin (*turning to look at her*) Intelligent, too. But I know what I'm doing, and there's no danger. I'm a fully qualified experimental investigator.

Mrs Hall Meaning what?

Griffin (*furiously*) Meaning I'm fully qualified to experimentally investigate!

Wicksteed (*to her; quietly*) A scientist. That's the new word for it.

Griffin Two brains? In Iping? On the same day? I—must write to *The Times*. (*He goes to the pub*) Just have it brought up. Don't come into my rooms. Leave it outside.

Mrs Hall I have to come in to clean.

Griffin No.

Mrs Hall What about the sheets?

Griffin Mrs Hall, my reason for coming here was a desire for solitude. The entry of a stranger into my rooms is not only a disturbance, it is a source of excruciating annoyance. In other words——

The music starts again as he crosses furiously towards her

—and to put it simply for *you*, Mrs Hall—I wish to be *left alone*!

The music softens as he turns towards Miss Statchell

There are, I'm sure, some here with the wit to understand such a yearning from someone in my position. (*He goes to the door. To Mrs Hall*) You have an easy remedy. If I'm a nuisance, load the bill.

He exits shutting the door

The music stops

Mrs Hall (*crossing* L; *calling after him*) Oh, I shall and don't you worry!

You get one day behind with your rent, and you'll be O.W.T! Out! (*She turns*) Glaring at me like an angry diving-helmet.

Fearenside moves DC, *staring in front like a madman*

Music

(*Becoming aware of Fearenside*) *Now* what's the matter with you?

Fearenside You saw what he did to me. You all saw. He ... *tweaked my nose*!

Burdock Don't be ridiculous. Fellow has no hand.

Miss Statchell Obviously, he *did* have an accident.

Fearenside I know what I'm talking about! I felt it! Something exactly like a finger and thumb—*nipped my nose*! And there wasn't anything there—not even the ghost of a hand! Well, you all saw it! (*He goes to the cart and throws out Griffin's belongings*) I'm not having anything to do with him! He can carry his own stuff up! I'm not going nowhere near him! Not for five pounds! Not for *ten* pounds! (*He wheels the cart*) Come on, Mafeking, we're going home!

The dog nods as Fearenside wheels the cart off UR

Burdock follows UL *to watch him go. The music stops*

Burdock Odd business.

Miss Statchell (*crossing slowly to the table and picking up her bag*) It's a fascinating mystery—and I'm sticking around until it's solved.

Burdock Aha! (*He hurries down to her left*) You see, Miss Statchell? (*He makes zz-ing noises and gestures from his head to hers*) Mind Control!

Miss Statchell Well, it's no' very likely to happen to *you*, Squire. Inbreeding has seen to that. Now where can I stay? That awful cottage is out of the question.

Mrs Hall You could try the vicarage. (*She indicates*) They often take people in.

Miss Statchell (*crossing* UL) Then I'll go there now.

Burdock (*keeping level with her,* UR) I could drop you.

Miss Statchell (*not even looking at him, as she goes*) Yes, Squire, why don't you do that?

She exits, UL

Burdock (*to Wicksteed; despondently*) Ah, well—better cancel the execution of that turkey, Wicksteed. (*He takes out his buttonhole*) It's only one for dinner—(*he tosses it away*)—again.

He exits, UR

Wicksteed (*following him*) I was afraid that might be the case, sir.

He exits, UR

Mrs Hall No wonder the aristocracy's in trouble. (*To Millie*) You! Take the 'eadless 'orseman's luggage upstairs. After all this excitement, I need a good lie-down.

A ripple of music as the gauze and blinder fly in, towers turn to arches both sides, the Light cross-fades to:

Scene 5

Burdock Has a Brain-wave

A Country Lane. A little later

Dappled light, birds twitter

Burdock enters L, *followed by Wicksteed*

Wicksteed I was merely venturing the opinion, sir, that Miss Statchell is a lady of political bent. Your mother would never approve.

Burdock (*stopping*) Wicksteed, I told you never to mention my mother again the last time you mentioned her!

Wicksteed I'm very sorry, sir.

Burdock My mother *never* approves of my lady-friends.

Wicksteed No, sir.

Burdock She doesn't even approve of *me* very much.

Wicksteed I'm afraid not, sir.

Burdock Don't ever mention her name in my presence again.

Wicksteed I won't, sir.

They continue R, *but there is a sudden musical ping as Burdock has a brain-wave, stopping*

Marvel pops on from L, *listening*

What is it, sir?

Burdock Something that chap said just now.

Wicksteed What was that, sir?

Burdock "Load the bill". Yet we know for a fact his bank account's empty.

Wicksteed So where will he find the money! Good thinking, sir.

Burdock Don't rub it in, Wicksteed. That was my intellectual ration for the day. Now it's back to the social grind. Let's go and shoot some trout, or something.

Wicksteed I think we're riding to hounds today, sir.

Burdock I've changed my mind, Wicksteed! It's one of the few things I'm allowed to do with it!

He exits, R

Wicksteed (*following him*) Well, it keeps your mother happy, sir.

He exits, R

Marvel moves C, *listening*

Burdock (*off*) Damn it, Wicksteed!

Wicksteed (*off*) Sorry!

Marvel (*to the audience*) You want to keep an eye on that Squire chappie. He's not as stupid as he looks. Well, you couldn't be, could you? And still a bachelor! Play your cards right, girls, and… Now, then: my favourite subject: me. After chopping Mrs Hall's wood, and being rewarded with a steaming pile of exquisitely-prepared turnips, I decided to roam around the Iping area for a while, sleep in the old dragon's wood shed, see if some other kind soul would feed me some proper grub. It was a bad mistake, but then—how was I to know that?

The blinder flies out as he crosses R, *pausing*

Oh, and by the way, that Squire chappie's on the right track: money *is* the clue to what happens next.

Harmonium is heard, played with one finger, badly, and Light bleeds through the gauze from the Vicarage

Ah, an organ! My favourite instrument.

He steps in the arch R, *and is revolved with it as the towers turn to two interior doors, the gauze rises, and Light fills from the front to:*

SCENE 6

Robbery at the Vicarage

The Vicarage. That night

At the rear, the curtains are open to the night sky. Either side of them, there are two niches containing busts. The Reverend Bunting—having cleaned the right bust—is heaving it back up to its place as Wadgers plays at the harmonium, L. *The bust crashes into place*

Wadgers Butterfingers.

Bunting You can talk. (*He sees Miss Statchell approaching* UL *and holds out his arms in welcome*) Ah, Miss Statchell!

She enters UL, *and Wadgers stops playing*

Miss Statchell Your wife's just given me tea, Vicar. I must say it's very decent of her.

Bunting Not at all. We're delighted to have you. (*He indicates*) This is Mr Wadgers, our Sexton.

Wadgers rises during this, and shakes Miss Statchell's hand. He finds her shake bone-crushing; she finds his limp and wet

He's staying with us tonight while his wife gives birth.

Wadgers Her seventh, actually. She's getting rather good at it, so I just let her get on with it.

Bunting (*to him*) *I'll* do the collection box, *you* do the candles.

Wadgers Rather.

They cross and sit at a work table, R, *their backs to her*

Miss Statchell (*after a pause; slightly taken aback at being so ignored*) I'd have stayed at the inn, but that strange man's taken over all the available rooms.

Bunting Yes, odd business, that.

Wadgers (*murmuring; cattily*) Odd about your cottage, too. The old schoolmistress professed herself perfectly comfortable there.

Miss Statchell Wasn't she blind?

Wadgers Well…

Miss Statchell Deaf too, I'm told.

Wadgers Only a little in one——

Miss Statchell They carted her off to the Poor House, didn't they?

Wadgers Well, her mind…

Miss Statchell (*sitting at the harmonium*) A lifetime of service brought her a pigsty and a pauper's grave. And yet—(*she plays the harmonium*)—this country she served has plenty of resources for small matters like caring for its old and needy. According to this new science fiction of Mr Wells, we'll soon be fighting a war with Martians, and flying to the moon. (*She finishes playing with a brilliant flourish, puts her pipe in her mouth, and turns to regard them*)

Bunting (*stiffly*) Charming nonsense, of course. It's quite impossible for man to go to the moon.

Wadgers Physically impossible.

Bunting The vacuum in the upper ether would compress the balloon.

Miss Statchell He seems awfully sure it'll happen one day.

Wadgers I prefer the views of my vicar. (*He places a hand on Bunting's shoulder*) Ronald has a wonderful sense for what is right. He particularly objects to these suffragettes.

Bunting If God had intended women to be equal, He would have created them so.

A banging, above. Both rise hastily

Oh, my word, it's the wife!

Wadgers She's anxious that we go to our rooms, Ronald. (*He crosses quickly* DR *and opens the door; to Miss Statchell*) May I escort you, Miss Statchell?

Miss Statchell (*crossing to him*) By all means, Sexton. I couldn't possibly attempt a flight of stairs without the aid of a gentleman.

She takes his candle from him, and exits

Wadgers Right. (*He hesitates, peers out into the darkness*)
Bunting Off you go, Wadgers. Sweet dreams.
Wadgers Yes. (*As he goes*) Oh, Miss Statchell, I wonder if I could ask you to——

He disappears with a yell and a crash, closing the door behind him

Bunting (*shaking his head as he picks up the cash box*) Seven children, and he can't find his way upstairs without a candle.

Singing "The Boy I Love", he crosses to the harmonium, looks around, hides the cash box in it, crosses back, picks up his candle, and turns off the lamp

He exits UL

A pause, then the drone is heard. A tapping at the window, then a crash, and bits of glass fall from below the lace curtains. Through them, we see the sash window rise up. The lace curtains are pushed aside, then—one after the other—the main curtains are closed. The tall stool shifts aside, and papers are moved and turned on the table. Drawers are opened and books thrown out. The empty collection box is thrown to the floor, etc., etc.

(*Off*) Hallo?

He enters UL, *wearing night-shirt and night-cap, carrying a candle*

Who's there? I know there's somebody, I heard you. (*He sees the mess*) Oh my word, the Church funds! (*He puts the candle on the table, hurries to the harmonium, and brings out the cash box*) Safe! Thank heavens for that. The Bishop would have had me crucified. (*He reaches for the candle*) I'll put them elsewhere.

The candle blows out. He reacts, staring at it. Then something grabs the cash box, pulling him to the table. He is thrown on his back, his arms drawn up and down as he fights to hang on to the cash box

He rises and runs off UL

Carrying a candle, Wadgers enters DR, *also wearing a night-shirt, followed by Miss Statchell in a night-dress*

Wadgers Ronald? What's going on?

Yelling, Bunting runs on from UL *and across and off* UR, *chasing the cash box, which floats in the air just out of his reach*

Wadgers runs to DL. *Bunting grabs the box and pulls it back on stage. He is thrown to the floor again. Wadgers goes to help, but the candle flies from his hand, and he doubles up, hit in the stomach. Bunting rises and is thrown down again. He runs to below the bust in the niche to the left of the window*

Bunting Wadgers! He's after the Church Funds!
Wadgers Who, Ronald?
Bunting Satan!
Wadgers Oh, my God! (*He runs to the work table to kneel and pray*)
Bunting No! *Satan!*

The bust is lifted from the niche and held high over his head

Miss Statchell Don't!

The bust turns to look at her

You'll kill him!

The bust is dropped, and Bunting catches it. The curtains are flung aside. All three run to the window to peer out. The sound of running feet crunching on gravel is heard. All downstage Light fades as the gauze and blinder fly in, the towers turn to wood shed R *and pub door* L, *and the Light cross-fades to:*

SCENE 7

A Silly Conversation

The Wood Shed. A few nights later

As the two towers complete their turn, Mrs Hall steps out of the wood shed, carrying a broom, and Jaffers steps out of the pub, helmet-less, carrying a beer

Pub piano is heard off: "Bird in a Gilded Cage"

Mrs Hall sweeps up any debris left from the Vicarage and puts it in the wood shed

Jaffers Nice drop of brew this, Mrs Hall. Very handy.

Mrs Hall Always willing to support the Constabulary, Mr Jaffers.

Jaffers *And* the Church, I see. You've got the Vicar in your saloon, writing a sermon on the demon drink. That can't be good for trade.

Mrs Hall I couldn't say no, Mr Jaffers, not after that awful affair down the Vicarage the other night. The poor soul's still got a huge bump on the side of his head.

Jaffers Ah, funny business, that. Never seen a burglary like it.

Mrs Hall (*closing the wood shed door*) Still no clues?

Jaffers Only these strange prints just outside the window that I'll swear were of bare feet. And on a freezing cold night, too. But we'll get him eventually. If at first you don't succeed—remember Bruce.

Mrs Hall (*crossing* L) Oh, that was a long time ago, Mr Jaffers. I don't see him no more.

Jaffers Who's that, Mrs Hall?

Mrs Hall Bruce Biggs. He was a nice enough lad, but nothing to a strapping chap like you.

Jaffers I was referring to Bruce and the Spider, Mrs Hall.

Mrs Hall (*after a pause*) No, he had a whippet and a gerbil.

The blinder flies out. Jaffers roars with laughter

Jaffers There're three things I like about you, Mrs Hall and one of 'em's your sense of humour.

He gooses her and chases her off into the pub, shrieking, closing the door

The Lights bleed through the gauze to where Burdock is sitting at the rustic table, melancholy, a tray of untouched food before him. The gauze flies out and the Lighting builds to:

SCENE 8

Jaffers Makes An Arrest

The Village Green. Same time

The shrieking continues; even Teddy's piano-playing is badly disturbed, but manages to come to a finish after Jaffers chases Mrs Hall from the rear of the pub, UL

They see the Squire, and react: Jaffers hurries back off UL *and returns with his helmet*

Mrs Hall fans herself L. *Jaffers crosses to Burdock*

Burdock Still on the job, Jaffers?
Jaffers I try to be, Squire. There are a lot of peculiar things going on at the moment. Sounds in empty rooms. Things going bump. Objects moving of their own accord.
Mrs Hall All that stuff flying around at the Vicarage.
Jaffers Footsteps running down the road when there's nobody there.
Mrs Hall Some people think we've got a ghost.
Jaffers It's right peculiar. But when you get down to it, what other explanation is there?

A cry and a crash of glass

Griffin (*off*) Go away!

They stare at the lighted window

Mrs Hall Oh, it's him again with the wrapped-up head. He just hates people in his rooms.

Griffin (*off*) I want to be left alone!

A crash

Millie flies out of the pub, clutching her broom

Millie He won't let me clean again, Mrs Hall. What shall I do?
Mrs Hall Just do the stairs and the landings. I'll sort him out later. (*She hesitates*) Well, go on, then!

Millie flies into the pub

The way some people behave. You're not safe in your beds.
Jaffers (*close*) You will be, Mrs Hall. The long arm of the law reaches everywhere. (*He indicates the bike*) I'll collect me bike later. (*To Burdock, as he goes*) Duty calls.

He exits, UR

Mrs Hall (*to Burdock*) If that bloke don't pop the question soon, I shall be obliged to look further afield.
Burdock Proposing to a lady's not that easy, Mrs Hall. (*He sighs*) If only it were.
Mrs Hall I need a man about the house, what with him upstairs.

As she indicates the lighted window, it goes out with a musical ping

D'you know, he's three weeks in arrears already. So I've had to tell him. In my hand by midnight, I said, or out you go first thing in the morning. That should see the back of him. There's nowhere he'll find any money this time of night.

Behind them, the pub door opens and closes softly. A sinister drone. Mrs Hall turns and moves towards it

Burdock What is it?
Mrs Hall This ghost they're talking about. (*She shivers*) I'm feeling an emanation myself. Unless I had too many pickled eggs last night.

Behind them, the bike straightens and is wheeled off UR, *the gears ticking. The drone ends on a tiny sting. Both react, turning to look* UR

What was that?

Burdock rises, goes to the exit UR, *and is about to peer off*

Miss Statchell (*off,* UL) Good-night, ladies!
Burdock (*turning*) It's *her*!
Miss Statchell (*off*) See you at the meeting!
Burdock (*to Mrs Hall*) Haven't you got any customers to serve, Mrs Hall?
Mrs Hall No, as it happens. But I can see I'm not wanted here. (*She opens the pub door*) Teddy! Get back on that piano! What do you think I pay you for?

She exits into the pub

Burdock rushes back to his chair and throws himself on it just as Miss Statchell enters UL

Pub piano: "Just a Song at Twilight"

Miss Statchell (*calling off behind her*) Don't be late now. (*She turns to regard the uncomfortable Burdock, one leg in his supper*) Waiting for *me*, were you, Squire?
Burdock No, no, just having a little pub supper.
Miss Statchell Outside? In this weather? You really shouldn't, you know. It's undignified. (*She puts the pipe in her mouth and makes for the pub door*)
Burdock Miss Statchell...! (*He jumps to his feet and goes to her*) I can't help myself! You don't seem to realize that once smitten with a lady, an English gentleman has only two options. He must win her affections, or——
Miss Statchell Go away somewhere to forget her. (*She puts a hand on his shoulder*) I believe a safari to far-off foreign parts is the usual recommendation.
Burdock Don't I know it? I've only recently returned from some filthy safari up the Amazon, trying to forget the *last* lady who rejected me. I've also been up the Congo, the Nile, the Zambezi, the Limpopo... Damn it, why does courtship have to be so difficult?
Miss Statchell (*putting her arm fully round him*) It's Nature's method for breeding an agreeable male—and she's still got a long way to go.

She finds him enjoying her close presence and pushes him away

Now behave yourself. I'm not entirely made of wood, you know.

A scream and a crash of broken glass. A sting. They react. A ring of a bicycle bell, and a yell from Marvel, off. A sting

Miss Statchell and Burdock run UL *to peer off* UR, *but Burdock leads Miss Statchell quickly to safety* DR, *before hurrying back* UL

Jaffers (*off*) Got you, me beauty!

A sting

Jaffers runs on from UR

I got him! I got him! And he ain't no ghost! So stand back—he's very dangerous!

A sting

He runs off, then returns dragging the manacled Marvel

Marvel I tell you I ain't done nothing!

Jaffers flings him to the ground DC. *A resolving sting*

Bunting—carrying a large ledger—and Wicksteed, come out of the pub

(*To the audience*) I said it'd be a big mistake to hang around here, madam.

Mrs Hall bursts out between Bunting and Wicksteed

Mrs Hall What is it? What's going on?
Burdock What's the meaning of this, Jaffers?
Jaffers (*taking out his notebook*) Robbery, sir. Post Office window smashed in, and a lot of money missing. A hundred quid in five-pound notes.

Miss Statchell And what makes you think this man's responsible?

Jaffers He's a tramp, miss.

Miss Statchell But did he *do* it?

Jaffers What, commit the actual offence, d'you mean? Well, I dunno. Does he *have* to have?

Marvel Listen——

Jaffers (*turning on him*) Speak when you're beaten up, otherwise keep quiet!

Burdock He *has* been beaten up.

Jaffers Self-inflicted, sir. That's how I found him, you see—lying in the road and pretending to groan. (*To Marvel*) You must think I'm stupid: there's no traffic this time of night.

A fast drone. The bicycle rides across the back, from R *to* L, *with a white bundle floating above the handlebars. A loud crashing and rolling of dustbins*

Burdock What the dickens was that?

Mrs Hall There's something in my dustbins!

All run up to peer off L, *except Marvel*

Marvel (*to the audience*) And it ain't rubbish, madam.

Jaffers It's my bicycle! Lying on its side, with the back wheel spinning! (*He stares at the pump*) But how'd it get there?

Marvel (*rising*) I been trying to tell you! This bloke on a bike ran right into me! (*He takes off a manacle, lifts his coat, and bends*) Look: tyre marks.

All run back, and crouch to examine the evidence

Burdock Seems pretty conclusive to me, Jaffers.

Mrs Hall (*to Marvel*) Well, who was it? Was he from round here?

Marvel (*slipping the manacle back on*) It's difficult to tell. It was dark, and—(*thoughtfully*)—now I come to think about it——

Short sinister drone

—he was a bit hard to see.

Very brief pause, then the sound of a terrible scream, off. All react. A big sting

Bunting Good Lord, what's that?

Another scream. Big sting

Mrs Hall It's Millie!

The Light snaps back on in the window with a ping

She's in *his* room! (*She hurries to the pub*) I *told* her not to go in there!

She goes into the pub

Miss Statchell (*pushing through the others*) Well, what are we standing here for? Let's see what's going on.
Burdock Good thinking. Follow me, chaps!

All hurry off L, *Jaffers contriving to be last*

Marvel Hey, hey, hey! (*He holds out his hands to Jaffers*) I been wrongfully arrested.
Jaffers Well, think yourself lucky we found out before we hanged you. (*He releases him*) Now hop it, or I'll do you for fun!

He runs off L

Percussion keeps tension going

Marvel Miserable git. He loves to see people suffer. Must be a Conservative. Hallo! A gourmet pub supper! (*He peers closer*) Untouched by human hands. Mrs Hall must have cooked it.

Another scream, and sting

(*Grabbing the pie*) I'm off out of here. (*To the audience, as he runs to exit*) I'll see you later, madam.

He runs off UR

Black-out

Segue from percussion to scene-change music. The blinder flies in, the towers turn to an arch R *and an interior door* L. *Millie takes her position. The Lights build on:*

Scene 9

Miss Statchell takes charge

Outside Griffin's Room. The same time

Millie is standing C, *clutching her broom, wailing, as the others run in from* R *to surround her: Bunting, Burdock and Wicksteed to her left; Mrs Hall, Miss Statchell, and Jaffers to her right*

Mrs Hall What is it? What's the matter with you? (*She pulls the broom off her*) Stop that awful wailing, and tell us what's wrong!
Wicksteed Allow me, madam.

He crosses to Millie, and slaps her. She stops. He continues the cross, to Miss Statchell

I used to be a male nurse in Johannesburg.
Millie Ooh, Mrs Hall, it was 'orrible—'orrible!
Mrs Hall *What* was 'orrible, you silly baggage?
Millie (*speaking very fast, drawing in shrieks of breath as required, each word clear but all too quick for them to understand*) Well—I was up here doing the landings like you told me to, when I see the door to *his* room—you know the funny one's——(*she indicates* L)

All snatch a quick look

—is open. So I think, well, if he ain't in there, I can do his room 'an all, so I go and have a look and right enough the room's empty, I'm really careful, Mrs Hall, I check everywhere, he ain't in there. So I start me sweeping and dusting, like, and while I'm at it, his window, the back one that looks out over the dustbins, sort of blows open all on its own, and in floats this weird funny-looking white shape!

Burdock (*baffled*) What did she say?

Wicksteed She says she was cleaning in the bandaged gentleman's rooms which were empty at the time, when a weird white shape floated in through the back window, sir—the one that overlooks the dustbins.

Burdock Good Lord!

Jaffers (*to Millie*) Well, what was it, woman? Some kind of ectoplasm?

Bunting Spirit manifestation?

Mrs Hall Astral body?

Burdock Albino bat?

Millie (*glaring at him*) It was *money*, sir! A bundle of five-pound notes!

Jaffers Hallo!

Millie Hanging in the air right in front of me eyes! There must have been a hundred quid!

Bunting I say!

Millie Then the door slams in me face, so I scream.

She puts a thumb in her mouth, and Mrs Hall comforts her. All stare at the door

Burdock (*slowly*) A hundred pounds worth of floating fivers, eh, Jaffers? You were wrong about that little tramp, but you were right about the guilty party not being a spook. He lives in *there*—(*indicating the door*) a certain johnny with his face missing.

Jaffers Well, we'll soon find out.

He crosses past them to the door, the others following. As he nears it, he slows, becoming more cautious, all bunching up behind him, except Miss Statchell who watches from R, *her arms folded. They go very close to the door, Jaffers putting his ear to it*

Burdock (*to Jaffers*) Well?

Jaffers jumps out of his skin, which makes everybody else do the same

Jaffers I'm proceeding, sir, I'm proceeding. (*He taps the door very softly with one knuckle. Almost inaudibly*) Open up, this is the Police. (*To Burdock*) Doesn't appear to be answering, sir.

Mrs Hall (*in a harsh whisper*) Mr Jaffers, if you ever want to speak to me again…!

Jaffers knocks on the door quickly and loudly

Griffin (*off*) Go away!

A big sting. All react back

Jaffers (*calling off*) I have reason to believe laws are being broken in there, sir.

Griffin (*off*) You inane village bumpkin! Laws are *made* to be broken! It's how we progress—by breaking laws our fathers thought immutable.

Millie What's he talking about?

Mrs Hall Shut up.

Millie And how did he get in there? The room was *empty*!

Mrs Hall Be *quiet*!

Burdock (*to Jaffers*) Why don't I pop back to the Hall and fetch my elephant gun. That'll soon persuade him.

Jaffers Allow a trained officer of the law to handle this, if you please, sir. (*He shouts off*) If you don't open this door, I shall lay my shoulder against it!

Griffin (*off*) You do, and I'll smash every bone in your body to a quivering jelly!

Jaffers (*after a pause, to Burdock*) Elephant gun, did you say, sir?

Miss Statchell (*impatiently*) Oh, let *me* try!

She pushes through the protesting group and knocks at the door

Do you mind if *I* have a word?

Griffin (*off*) Who is it?

Miss Statchell We met outside. You said you'd like to get to know me better.

Griffin (*off, after a brief pause*) Just you, then. But I warn you—if anybody else tries to get in, I'll turn violent—and you have little idea how perilous that can be.

Miss Statchell Only me, I promise. Unlock the door. (*She gives her handbag to Burdock*) I'll find out what I can, then ask him to let you in.

Burdock Damn it, he might be dangerous.

Wicksteed The young lady seems to know what she's doing, sir. We can always break in if we have to.

Burdock All the same, I really do think——

Miss Statchell (*putting her hat on him*) What with?

The sound of a bolt

Jaffers He's unlocked it. (*To the others*) We'll just give her five minutes. (*To Miss Statchell*) D'you hear that, miss? Five minutes, then we're coming in after you.
Miss Statchell (*putting her pipe in Burdock's mouth*) Very well. Now just wait out *here*.

Black-out, scene-change music

The company slip off between the cloth and the tower

The music stops, and we hear the sound of Miss Statchell closing the door as the blinder rises on:

Scene 10

The Unveiling of the Stranger

Griffin's Room. The same time

Miss Statchell is closing and locking the door, the knob now on the other side, the Light filling from the front

The room is filled with bubbling equipment on the table R, *a swivel chair* L *with its back turned to Miss Statchell, books and an oil-lamp on the floor* C. *Black material covers the curtains in the upstage alcove; there is genial disorder, everything pushed back to the walls so that Griffin can work on the floor* C

Jaffers (*off*) Only five minutes now, miss.
Miss Statchell Yes, yes, I heard you the first time, Constable. Now just do as you're told, and wait out *there*. (*She moves into the room, surveys it. She picks up the lamp, and puts it on the table*) Hallo? Are you there? It's only me.

The chair swivels, and Griffin faces her, smoking. He wears a dressing gown, scarf, gloves, and the usual bandages and glasses. A big sting

You made me jump.

Griffin Is that all?

Miss Statchell It's not important.

Griffin No, it isn't. (*He stubs out his cigarette*) Those fools out there do more than make me jump, Miss Statchell. They make me blind with rage.

Miss Statchell They're only curious.

Griffin *I have a right to my privacy!* It's been one long stream of interferences ever since I arrived! (*He mimics*) "I'm 'ere to mend the clock, zor"... "Would 'ee like a nice cup of tea, zor?" Fearenside and that damned dog...! I'd like to shoot the lot of them.

Miss Statchell You don't mean that.

Griffin (*turning the chair more*) I'll show you.

She flinches

You draw back.

Miss Statchell I try not to. It's your——

Griffin My—affliction? Is that the fascination? If so, you're no better than the others. (*He turns the chair away again*)

Miss Statchell It's only natural.

Griffin (*rising and appearing from behind the chair*) It's also natural that a man with *this* would wish to be left in peace!

Miss Statchell (*gently*) How did it happen to you?

Griffin I—had an accident with an experiment. A process that was supposed to be reversible went wrong. I couldn't go back. (*He kneels by the books*) Now I'm searching for the cure.

Miss Statchell I don't understand. It disfigured you in some way?

Griffin Disfigured? (*With grim amusement*) Yes, I suppose you could call my problem "disfigurement".

Music underlays

There were two of us—both chemists. Myself, and a doctor called Kemp. Only Kemp turned out to be a bit of a disappointment. He wanted to steal my idea, keep it all to himself.

Miss Statchell So what did you do?

Griffin We had a disagreement, and there was a fire. Everything went up in smoke—including my notebooks. I had to re-create the whole experiment from scratch.

Miss Statchell That must have been difficult.

Griffin (*sneering at the paltriness of the word*) *Difficult?* (*He rises, holds one notebook, moving* DL) To re-create one's life's work? Yes, it was *difficult*. But then, I'm accustomed to that. My life has been one long *difficulty*. Always on the outside, never let in, never invited, never encouraged… Oh yes, I know all about *difficulty*.

Jaffers (*off, knocking*) Two minutes, miss!

The music stops

Griffin (*going to the door*) Shut up! Go away!

Miss Statchell crosses quickly to the chair

The brazen fools! (*He crosses to the table, studying the notebook*) I must have peace to work! Time to find the solution! (*He holds up a beaker, turning his back on her, lifting his glasses to examine it*) But that's not it! (*He hurls it off,* UR, *where it shatters*) Wrong, again! Failure after failure! (*He sweeps objects off the table and buries his head in his hands*)

Burdock (*off*) Miss Statchell, are you all right?

Miss Statchell (*going to the door*) Yes, yes, I'm fine! Leave us alone! It was my fault, I knocked something over. (*She turns to look at him*) He's all right.

Soft music underlays. He lifts his head, turns slowly to look at her

Griffin You could share with me…

Miss Statchell Share what?

Griffin Power. You've no idea of the power in this thing. We could order a whole new world—the shape of things to come.

Miss Statchell Why me?

Griffin (*crossing slowly to her*) You're different. I knew it the first time we met. And ever since then, I've been observing you—closely—more closely than you realize. You must understand this—makes relationships difficult—and I miss it… I miss it dreadfully.

The music stops

Jaffers (*off, hammering*) Time's up, miss! We're coming in!

Griffin (*staring wildly about him*) So close, so close, nearly there, if only they'd leave me alone. Why won't they leave me alone? Curse them! They'll pay! I'll make them pay!
Jaffers (*off*) Get your shoulder to it!
Mrs Hall (*off*) Here, what about the damage?
Burdock (*off*) Hang the damage! This is an emergency.

Griffin feverishly collects up his notebooks

Griffin They mustn't see these notebooks! Hold them off! Make them go away!
Miss Statchell (*calling off*) You've got to give us more time!
Jaffers (*off*) No chance, miss!

A crash at the door

Griffin hurries off, UL

A second crash

On the third crash, all spill in, Jaffers and Burdock first, then Mrs Hall and Millie, then Bunting and Wicksteed

Mrs Hall (*pushing through to* C) What's he been doing to my room? My furniture—it's ruined!
Millie (*crossing to the table*) He's trying to put you out of business, Mrs Hall. Look—he's brewing his own beer.
Mrs Hall (*joining her*) What?
Jaffers (*to Miss Statchell,* DC) Where is he?
Miss Statchell Find him yourself.
Mrs Hall (*indicating the door* DR) He must be in the bedroom.
Jaffers (*to Miss Statchell*) Excuse me, miss.

A pause, then she moves upstage

Thank you, sir. (*He crosses to the door*) Are you in there, sir? If so, I must ask you to reveal yourself. (*After a pause*) Failure to reveal yourself to a policeman upon request can result in very serious consequences.

Griffin It already *has*!

The chair spins, and Griffin is there as before, smoking. A big sting. All draw back

What do you mean by bursting into a man's private rooms?

Mrs Hall They're your rooms so long as you pay for 'em, and that you haven't done for weeks.

Griffin I told you I'd get it, and I have. Here—(*he tosses a bundle of notes in front of them*) help yourself.

Millie (*jumping up and down in excitement, pointing*) That's it, that's it! The weird white shape!

Mrs Hall (*heavy with significance*) *Fivers*, Mr Jaffers.

Jaffers Hallo! (*He picks them up and moves* UC) And I wonder where you found *them*, sir.

Griffin (*furiously*) What do you mean?

Mrs Hall He means he wonders where you found 'em. And before I take a penny, I should like to ask you to explain some things what I don't understand, what nobody don't understand, and what we're all very anxious to understand.

Jaffers If I could just caution him, Mrs Hall...

Mrs Hall I'd like to know what you've been doing with my furniture, I'd like to know what you've been doing in here that you have to hang up them black curtains to hide it, and most of all I'd like to know what you're doing in a room what was empty a minute ago.

Jaffers (*to Griffin*) It is my duty to warn you——

Mrs Hall It is a rule of this house that them that stays in the house comes into the house by way of the doors provided in the house! They are not permitted to de-materialize through the bleeding walls!

Gradually a free-for-all argument develops:

Jaffers Mrs Hall, I'm trying to carry out an arrest here.

Mrs Hall I'm only putting my point of view.

Burdock (*moving to* C) Very ably, too.

Mrs Hall (*turning on him*) And you can shut your 'ead, an' all! It was you what broke my best door!

Miss Statchell (*moving* DR) I told them not to come in.

Wicksteed (*he crosses to her*) We *had* to, miss.

Burdock (*going to her*) It was all that banging and crashing...
Millie (*crossing down to her*) He might have been dismemberin' you.
Bunting (*crossing to her*) Like in the Red Barn.
Miss Statchell Oh, don't be ridiculous!

Jaffers moves down to left of the group, vainly trying to quell the argument

Griffin (*cracking*) *Shut up, the lot of you!*

A big sting. All react into a tight group DR

You haven't a clue what I am, yet you barge in here and take me over! Well, by heaven, then, you deserve the truth, and you shall have it! Here! (*He throws his glasses at them*)

A sting

Here! (*He takes the bandaged top of his head off—like a skull-cap—and throws it at them*)

A sting

And—(*he unwinds the rest of the bandages and throws them at them*) here!

A sting. Sinister drone continues

Now are you satisfied?

Pause

Mrs Hall Oh, my gawd, he ain't got no 'ead.

Griffin puts a cigarette to the space where his mouth is, and draws. The tip glows, smoke is expelled

Millie I'm getting out of here.

She goes to run but Jaffers places himself quickly before the group

Jaffers Just a minute, just a minute...! (*He turns to Griffin*) 'Ead or no 'ead, I'm 'ere to make an arrest, and arrest you I will.

Griffin (*puffing*) Is there a charge?

Mrs Hall Course there's a charge! You ain't got no 'ead!

Griffin That's illegal, is it? Unlicensed headlessness? Decapitated conduct? Appearing only partially in a public place?

Jaffers I may be a simple village copper, sir, but I know an offence when I see one, and you're committing it. (*He moves* UC *and takes out his handcuffs*) Take off those gloves and hold out your hands.

Griffin By all means.

He puts down the cigarette, pulls off the gloves, tosses them at Jaffers. Jaffers stares at the empty sleeves a moment, then crosses down to the group

Jaffers Bit of a poser here, sir. If he ain't got no 'ands, I can't cuff him, and if he ain't got no 'ead I can't whack him with me truncheon. These are the only arrest procedures I know.

Miss Statchell We don't know he's done anything to *be* arrested!

Jaffers We suspect it, miss, and that's good enough in this country. (*He looks at Griffin and lowers his voice still further*) Here's what I suggest, sir. I'll keep him occupied in intelligent discourse while you and Mr Wicksteed sneak up behind him and nab him.

Burdock *We're* going to sneak up behind him while *you* keep him occupied in intelligent discourse?

Jaffers Yes, sir.

Burdock (*to Wicksteed, with some irony*) There's something wrong with this plan, but I can't quite put my finger on it. (*To Jaffers*) Very well, discourse away. We'll do our stuff.

Jaffers turns to Griffin, takes off his helmet and begins putting glasses and bandages into it

Jaffers (*to Griffin*) Now then, sir, why don't we try being reasonable?

Griffin Sounds reasonable.

Jaffers (*crossing to the chair against the wall* L) I realize being 'eadless must make it difficult for a chap to concentrate, but I'd like you to listen most carefully to what I have to say. (*He puts down the helmet and sits*)

Meanwhile, Burdock and Wicksteed are slipping along the edge of the table to UC

Griffin With what?
Jaffers Pardon?
Griffin With what shall I listen?
Jaffers Well, with your—erm——
Griffin Come to that, how am I talking to you?
Jaffers Why, through your—erm——
Griffin You see, Constable, you're out of your depth. *All* of me is like this.
Jaffers I don't get you, sir.
Griffin The fact is, I'm invisible. It's a confounded nuisance, but is it any reason for you to persecute me?
Jaffers You're a rum customer, and no mistake. (*He leans back in the chair*) But I'm enjoying our little chat—(*he crosses one leg on his knee*) so why don't we continue?

Griffin crosses the same leg

Tell me about this "invisibility"—— (*He swaps his legs over*)

Griffin does the same

—Is it like mumps? (*He puts both feet on the ground*)

Griffin does the same

In the background, Burdock is silently counting to three on his fingers to Wicksteed

Could *I* catch it?

Burdock and Wicksteed now turn to pounce, but Miss Statchell snatches up the lamp

Miss Statchell (*running* C) Look out!

She blows out the lamp, and the room becomes very dim. Griffin spins the chair to face upstage, and Burdock and Wicksteed recoil. Jaffers rises and runs to the chair, L. *Miss Statchell runs* DL

Bunting Careful with that lamp, Miss Statchell!
Burdock (*running after her*) What are you doing?

Miss Statchell (*to Griffin*) Run!

A sting, and the headless Griffin runs up into the window alcove

Griffin I don't have to, Miss Statchell! These fools can't hurt me! But they've asked for it, and here it comes!

He throws his scarf at Mrs Hall, who picks it up. A sting

I gave you your chance! Now you'll pay! (*He turns upstage and begins to slip out of his dressing-gown*)

Millie Here, what's he doing?

Mrs Hall Shut up!

Griffin (*turning front*) You're all so interfering! Reap your reward!

He throws his dressing-gown at Mrs Hall, who picks it up. A sting

Wicksteed (*running to* C) Millie—fetch another lamp from the bar! Quickly!

She runs out DL

Wicksteed moves UR

Griffin Wouldn't believe me, would you? Thought I was fooling! Well, now you know! And what do you think? Eh? Eh?

His night-shirt cavorts, cackling with laughter. Xylophone

Wicksteed (*crossing quickly to Burdock*) We've got to stop him, sir! Once he gets all of his clothes off…!

Mrs Hall We won't be able to see where he is!

Bunting He could do *anything*!

Burdock Constable Jaffers!

Jaffers runs to him and salutes

Jaffers Sir?

Burdock (*indicating*) Arrest that shirt!

Jaffers Right you are, Squire!

He runs up and grapples with it

Burdock And whatever you do, don't let go! (*He runs* L) Where's that lamp?

Millie (*off*) Coming, Squire!

She runs into the room and across to the table with the lamp

Lighting is restored, and Jaffers moves DC, *fighting with an empty shirt. Millie puts the lamp down. The music stops*

Burdock You fool, Jaffers!

Jaffers I had him a minute ago, sir! I *felt* him! He's got to be in here somewhere!

A low laugh from Griffin

He *is* in here somewhere.

Bunting Oh, my word…

Sinister drone. Jaffers tosses the shirt on the chair, pokes about with his truncheon, the others feeling the air all around them, almost in slow motion. A moment or two, then—in turning—Wicksteed sees the open door

Wicksteed The door, sir!

He runs to it, shuts it, and begins to drag a heavy packing case across in front of it

Burdock Good thinking, Wicksteed. We'll never catch him outside.

Mrs Hall Never mind about catching him.

They feel a little more. Suddenly, Millie shrieks and jumps. Music. All turn to stare at her. Burdock cries out, feeling his cheek. Music. All stare at him. Then, in rapid succession, Bunting, Jaffers and Mrs Hall are poked and prodded, Mrs Hall having her foot stepped on, hopping to C, *joined by Bunting*

Oh Vicar, Vicar! We're all in mortal danger!

Griffin (*close*) And not only *mortal*, Mrs Hall... There's a fate worse than death.

Her large breasts begin to bob up and down vigorously as she shrieks. Music. It stops, and she holds them still

Mrs Hall The man's a sex maniac! He's interfered with my bodice. (*She shrieks, feels her behind, and crosses quickly* DL) And my bum! (*Indignantly*) If my Albert were alive...!

Griffin If your Albert were alive, he'd be over here, giving *this* little lady a lift.

Millie is lifted high in the air. Music

Millie (*struggling*) Ooh, Mrs Hall, tell him to put me down! I got no 'ead for 'eights!

Jaffers pokes his truncheon around and above Millie, searching for Griffin, but missing the obvious position until it's too late: immediately in front of her

Griffin 'Ave you got an 'ead at all, that's the question. However, down you come.

She is lowered to music. During the following, Jaffers realizes his mistake, pokes in front of her: too late. He pulls her aside, staring at the emptiness all around her

Mustn't tease little girls. I'm after bigger game. (*He laughs*)

Mrs Hall shrieks again

Mrs Hall Ow! He's at it again! Where is he? (*She lifts her skirts and peers underneath. She wears rather odd underwear*)

Burdock (*adopting a boxing stance*) You filthy blighter! Leave the women alone, and come out and fight like a man!

Griffin Certainly.

The sound of a blow, and Burdock is knocked flat, unconscious, DRC

Miss Statchell…

Miss Statchell (*nervously*) Yes?

She is pulled close to him, ULC

(*Fighting for her breath*) Is this the shape of things to come? Taking advantage of helpless women?

Jaffers pokes his truncheon behind her: wrong again

Griffin Helpless?

She is turned to face Mrs Hall

Look at her: she's about as helpless as a sledgehammer.

In the background, Jaffers signals to the others, indicating Griffin's obvious position, and urges them to form a circle round it, arms outstretched

However, you're right.

She is pushed, gently but firmly, aside UL, *where—seeing what is going on—she joins the circle*

Time for these silly games to end. I must leave.

In quick succession, the circle of people is disposed of: Burdock is socked on the jaw again, to collapse DRC; *Bunting is smacked on the nose, reacting* DR; *Millie is pushed* UR; *Jaffers doubles up with a blow to the stomach, staggering back* UC; *Miss Statchell and Wicksteed are pushed* UL; *Mrs Hall thrown across* R. *The case of books is dragged aside, and the door opens. Wicksteed recovers and grabs Griffin in the doorway, dragging him back to* UC

Wicksteed I've got him, sir! Give me a hand, someone!

Jaffers I'll soon see to him.

He aims a mighty blow with his truncheon, but Griffin turns Wicksteed, who receives it, collapsing into Miss Statchell's arms. She seats him L, *ministering to him during the following*

Bunting You idiot, Jaffers!
Jaffers Just doing my duty, sir.

He hears a movement from Griffin

Aha! (*He aims another blow*)

A clonk and a cry from Griffin

I got him, I got him! (*He pokes about on the floor for the body*)
Griffin You stupid policeman!

The truncheon flies from Jaffers's hand

You'll die for that!

Jaffers is throttled by invisible hands

You're a dead man, you fool.
Miss Statchell (*still ministering to Wicksteed; to Griffin*) Stop it! You're killing him!
Griffin (*between his teeth*) I mean to be, my dear.
Jaffers (*forcing the invisible hands apart*) Not tonight, you don't! (*He sees a knife on the table, snatches it up, and slashes around the room*)

Music throughout

Burdock (*on the floor*) Careful, man! You'll cut the ladies!
Mrs Hall Never mind about us, Mr Jaffers!
Millie Just get him!
Wicksteed (*holding his head*) Give him one for me, Jaffers!
Jaffers (*saluting him*) I will, Mr Wicksteed, sir——

He is yanked to C, *as his knife-holding hand is grabbed by Griffin*

—ah!

He tackles Griffin, and strains, apparently on top

(*Triumphantly*) Ah, ha!

His face changes as the music changes also and the knife begins to turn in towards his neck

Oh, oh. (*He strains desperately*) Ah... Ah... (*The knife eventually pierces his neck*) Aaagh! (*He collapses, apparently dead*)

Mrs Hall (*going to him, kneeling*) Oh, Mr Jaffers...

Miss Statchell moves in a little, then gives a sudden gasp as Griffin takes her, turning her upstage

Griffin Thank you for trying to help. We'll meet again one day.

She is kissed and released, feeling her mouth

Meanwhile—Iping's too small for the Invisible Man!

Papers scatter, the curtains bulge outwards, there is a huge smash of breaking glass. Burdock and Bunting run to the window, and pull down the black curtains. There is a gaping hole in the window in the shape of a man. A small piece tinkles down. Music. The Lights fade to Black-out

The CURTAIN *falls*

ACT II

Scene 1

Setting the Scene

On the stage

Music. The Curtain *rises, and the MC bounds on stage*

MC And now, ladies and gentlemen—enticingly exhibited by our most eminent employee here at the Empire—meaning that marvellous man, the MC, me, myself—and after a perfect pint of pristine porter personally poured by the proprietor to pacify my pride—we present—at even more *enormous expense*—part two, three, four...

He goes off L *and the Ladies dance on from* R

Song 2: Who's There?

All (*singing*) Oh, here we are, it's Freda and her Follies once again
Ladies There's two of us is ladies
Freda And the rest is only men
All We play our parts so perfectly you'll wonder who is which
We sometimes get ourselves confused, which causes quite a hitch

The men enter from R

Men It's time to carry on and show you all what's coming next
We'll take the parts we took before or you'll be all perplexed
Ladies Occasionally the things we do may strike you as uncouth
Men But Mr Marvel swears that what is happening is the truth

All Drink your coffee, put your sweets away, it's time to start again

Soon the story will continue, all the lights go down, and then…

The House Lights go out. They whisper

Who's there? What was that? It's him! He's very near!
You never see him coming but you always know he's here

Shut the door and say your prayers because the time is coming when
You'll be seeing something awfully strange and you'll be wondering then…
Is it? If it is, don't be too afraid…

The two ladies go off R *during the following, returning with a log, which they put down*

Our story now is moving to a pretty forest glade
And what on earth can happen in a pretty forest glade?

With knowing looks, winks, tapping their noses significantly, they go out, R

At the same moment, Marvel enters L

The Lights cross-fade to:

Scene 2

His First Disciple

A Forest Glade. The following day

The Light is dappled, and birds twitter as Marvel, mopping his face with a handkerchief, sits on the log

Marvel (*to the audience*) Me again—your sophisticated raconteur. D'you enjoy the shindig last night? When the Invisible Man tickled Mrs

Hall's wotsits? Wish *I'd* seen it, but I'd run off long before. So here I am, the next day, knowing nothing about any Invisible Man, just about to settle down and partake of this sustenance I appropriated… (*He takes a pie from the bundle*) Eat this food I nicked, madam… When I discovered my big mistake. Settling down. I should have run for miles.

Griffin Talking to yourself, old man?

Marvel stares about him, and his shoulder is thumped

Answer me when I'm speaking to you!

Marvel All right, all right. But don't hit me *too* hard; I might wake up.

Griffin Oh, so you think you're dreaming.

Marvel Well, I hope so, 'cos otherwise you'd have to be a ghost.

Griffin Why not?

Marvel's stick flies up and belabours his head

Woo...!

Marvel Oy! Oy! (*He catches it and rises*) Where are you?

Griffin Here.

Marvel yells and jumps as he is pinched

Marvel Ow! What you doing?

Griffin I'm pinching you, Marvel.

Marvel Pinching me? (*He covers himself*) Hey, hey, watch it!

Griffin Do calm down, old chap, and take a seat.

Marvel goes to sit, but his log is kicked over and he collapses. He staggers up, righting the log

Marvel You've got a bloody marvellous act, I'll tell you that. Where are you? Up a tree?

Griffin No! Can't you grasp what's in front of you?

Marvel is pulled L *by his nose*

Marvel (*through his nose*) Can't I grasp what's in front of me?

Griffin An Invisible Man is pulling your nose.

Marvel (*through his nose*) An Invisible Man is pulling my nose?
Griffin (*releasing him*) I'm right in front of you, and you can't see me. Allow me to introduce myself.

Marvel's hand is pumped up and down

I'm the Invisible Man.

Marvel's hand is released

Marvel Invisible Man?
Griffin Yes.

The sound of Griffin's voice now comes from R *and Marvel turns to stare*

Marvel Then it was *you* did that job down the Post Office!
Griffin Worse than that. I've killed a policeman.
Marvel Oh, a reformer as well as a robber. Which policeman?
Griffin Jaffers, in the village.
Marvel I wish you had. The man's a pest.
Griffin (*taken aback*) I stuck a knife in his throat.
Marvel Unfortunately, the Squire's gentleman also used to be an ambulance man in Amsterdam, and stemmed the bleeding—so you ain't killed nobody.
Griffin Oh. Well, I nearly killed *you*.
Marvel D'you what?
Griffin I was wandering—naked—impotent—mad with fury at the stupidity of people—and there you were. I came up behind you—hesitated—went on—stopped.
Marvel I was just beginning to enjoy this story. Why didn't you keep on going?
Griffin To where?

He brushes past Marvel, upstage of him, to L

If I can't win in a tiny place like Iping, how can I hope to take on the world? Here, I said, is an outcast—like myself. He can be my first disciple. So I came back.
Marvel Disciple? I'm all over dizzy. How can I help?

Griffin Come for a stroll, and we'll have a chat.

Marvel's arm is taken and he is walked back and forth

I can do wonderful things, but not simple things. I can walk into a bank and help myself, but the money stays visible, and I'm vulnerable. On the other hand, if I had some assistance... I don't have to spell out the rewards...

Marvel (*released to fall into his seat*) Why not?

Griffin But as I grow in power, so shall my disciples... And you shall be the first. But should you fail me...

Marvel's collar is lifted

Is my meaning conveyed?

Marvel Lord, yes.

Griffin Then gather up your things. I have a task for you. I left so quickly last night, I had to abandon all my notes. After we recover them, we'll seek out my old collaborator, Dr Kemp. He's a poor tool, but I also require *skilled* assistance.

Marvel (*looking longingly on his pie*) Couldn't I finish me pie first?

Griffin By all means. Let me help you.

It is pushed into his face

You're mine now, and that means do as you're told!

Marvel is dragged to his feet

This way!

He is dragged to exit L

We have to save my sanity, Marvel—because if I lose it, God help you all!

Scene-change music and Black-out. Fly out blinder, strike log, turn towers to two interior doors

Scene 3

Trouble at the Inn

The Saloon Bar. A little later

The Light bleeds through the gauze to reveal Miss Statchell seated on the piano stool, making notes. Bunting is on a stool, R, *slumped; Wicksteed at the high bar stool, reading notebooks*

Sound of a crowd off

Burdock forces his way into the bar as the gauze rises, and the Light fills from the front

Burdock (*calling off*) Sorry. Can't tell you a thing. My lips are sealed. (*He shuts the door*) Good job Colonel Adye shut the saloon. Keeping this thing secret's dashed difficult.

Miss Statchell Even impossible. I'm writing a report for the evening papers.

Bunting (*jolted*) I say, Miss Statchell! We were asked to keep it under wraps, don't you know.

Miss Statchell Sorry, but I believe in freedom of information.

Burdock (*reeling*) Freedom of information? Good God!

Bunting You can't run a country if people know how it's done.

Burdock They think there's a trick to it.

Colonel Adye enters DL, *closing his notebook*

Adye (*calling off behind him*) Well, you should have gone before you left the station. (*He closes the door and crosses* UC. *To Bunting*) That's as much as we can do today. Where's the landlady?

Bunting Preparing us a pot of tea, Colonel. We need it.

Adye Yes, it's all rather unbelievable. Jaffers injured in the line of duty. (*To Wicksteed*) That tourniquet you put round his neck, sir, saved his life.

Wicksteed Normally, there'd be a danger of brain damage, but—(*he looks up at them*) under the circumstances…

All Yes, yes, quite.

Adye Rum do. (*To Wicksteed*) I'll want to have a look at those books when you've finished. You never know—there might be a clue in 'em.

Burdock What are they, exactly?

Wicksteed The Invisible Man's notebooks, sir. I used to be a cryptographer in St Petersburg, and Colonel Adye asked me to look them over, but they're a bit tricky.

Burdock (*strolling over*) Oh? Some sort of code?

Miss Statchell (*taking the pipe from her mouth*) Mathematics. So I suppose it *would* be code to *you*, Squire.

Burdock Insult me all you like, Miss Statchell. I'll soon be out of your hair—trying to forget all about you on another infernal safari.

Wicksteed (*to her*) In India, I regret to say.

Burdock Yes, it's up the Ganges, this time. (*Over Wicksteed's shoulder*) And what's the problem here? FX equalling X squared minus two is only a boring old polynomial.

Wicksteed Yes, sir, but he goes on to factor it, and that's not allowed.

Burdock It is if the coefficients are real numbers, and since X squared minus two equals X plus the square root of two, and the square root of two is not rational, it follows that any polynomial with complex coefficients may be factored into linear polynomials, provided a lesser coefficient domain is not specified. (*He becomes aware of stares and stillness in the room, and tries to pass it off with a laugh*) Sorry about that. Wicksteed's my old tutor, and we sometimes forget. Not to worry. (*He indicates his head*) Brain of a newt. (*He burbles his lips, then suddenly turns to look at the door*)

Adye What is it?

Burdock Odd sort of noise outside. (*He opens the door and peers out*) It's all right, it's only that little tramp. (*He takes a second look*) Must have had an accident. He's running this way with his arm twisted up his back.

Mrs Hall (*off*) Tea, everybody!

Bunting Oh, jolly good!

Burdock shuts the door

Millie enters, carrying a large tray with cups, plates, cake, and a bread knife on it. She is followed by Mrs Hall, bearing a large brown metal catering teapot

Mrs Hall Put it on the table, Millie. It's under the tray.

Millie puts it down, and stands to Mrs Hall's left as Mrs Hall pours, singing

Bunting You're remarkably cheerful this morning, Mrs Hall.

During the following, Millie turns past Bunting and Adye to give tea to Miss Statchell

Mrs Hall And why wouldn't I be? I've just come from visiting Mr Jaffers, and he agreed to everything I said. We may soon be announcing a happy event.
Miss Statchell (*taking her tea*) I thought his larynx was severed, and he couldna speak.
Mrs Hall (*very firmly*) Silence is assent, that's what I always say.
Bunting Still, after that terrible night...
Mrs Hall Oh, mass 'allucination, that's all that was. Collective 'ypnosis. Millie read about it.
Millie (*taking a second cup of tea*) It was in *True Life Detective Stories*. (*She takes tea past Bunting to Adye, returning during the following to take tea to Burdock and then Wicksteed, on both occasions turning towards Bunting first*)

Mrs Hall begins cutting the cake with the bread knife

Mrs Hall Yes—(*with relish*) *The Case of the Master Criminal* who's got powers of the mind and eyes like twin pools of spinning darkness.
Millie He escapes justice by 'ypnotizing people into believing he's not there.
Mrs Hall When all the time he is.
Adye (*helping himself to the cake and crossing* DL) I must admit I've been considering something similar myself.
Miss Statchell *What?* You think he fooled us all? We didn't see what we saw?

Millie takes a cake past Bunting to Miss Statchell

Burdock Saw what we didn't see, actually.
Miss Statchell Button your lip.

She takes the cake from Millie. Mrs Hall takes a cake to Burdock and

Wicksteed. Millie picks up the knife, and licks it. It will have escaped nobody that Bunting got neither tea nor cake

Adye My dear young lady, there has to be a rational explanation.

Miss Statchell Ay! The man's made himself invisible! What will it take to convince you? An affidavit from God, countersigned by George Washington?

Millie puts the knife on the barrel and dusts the piano in a desultory sort of way

Mrs Hall Ooh… (*"hark at her", and sits at the stool,* R)

Adye People who've been taken in always like to hang on to their delusions, miss. I remember this chap who bought Tower Bridge——

Miss Statchell (*rising*) Don't waste your breath! (*She puts her tea and cake back on the tray*) I spoke with the man in his room. (*She returns for her bag*) He's full of the most abnormal exasperation—(*she crosses to Adye*) he simply burns with rage at the merest provocation——

Millie sits on the piano stool

—but I'm certain he's no charlatan—(*she crosses up to the door*) and I hope to meet him again one day.

Millie Watch out for his eyes, miss.

Miss Statchell Don't be a fool, Millie.

Mrs Hall No need to take it out on her.

Millie Yes, there's no need to take it out on me.

Mrs Hall (*to her*) Shut up.

Miss Statchell He needs understanding—and that's a rare commodity around here!

She goes out, slamming the door

Adye (*disapprovingly*) Forthright young woman, that.

Burdock (*approvingly*) Isn't she, though?

Adye (*crossing to above the table, putting down his cup and helping himself to more cake*) Well, we'll continue our enquiries. At least his notebooks have put a name to him.

Wicksteed Yes… Griffin… Rather appropriate his being named after such a fabulous creature. And there's also another name here... A minor collaborator not privy to the main secret, but involved in some way. He's mentioned in a cryptic reference to a fire...

Music underlays

"You believe me dead, but one day I shall rise from the ashes, a Phoenix become Nemesis—*your* Nemesis, Dr Kemp".

Music stops

Bunting Kemp?
Adye (*to Bunting*) That name familiar to you, sir?
Bunting There's a London doctor of that name with a country house a few miles outside the village...
Adye Well, if he's involved, we'll soon find out. (*He helps himself to more cake. To Wicksteed*) I'll pick up the books later. (*He opens the door*)
Mrs Hall (*to him*) No wonder you're so fat.
Adye Sergeant, clear this riff-raff...!

He exits and closes the door after him

Mrs Hall (*to Millie, handing her a glass of milk with a straw*) And you—drink your milk.

During the following, Millie sniffs it, pulls a face and puts it on the piano

Burdock (*sitting at the stool* L) He thinks we saw an illusion. Mirrors, or something.
Bunting If only it were true.
Burdock The Amazing Invisible Man. (*He sips tea*) Well, however he did it, he won't be coming *here* again. We can write "closed" to this extraordinary episode. It's over. Ended. Finished. Done with. Run its course. Terminated.

Marvel suddely enters

Marvel Excuse me.

All jump out of their skins

Is this the Public Bar?

Mrs Hall (*recovering*) No. And don't come in here in your muddy boots.

Marvel Sorry. (*He sees the books and becomes alert*)

A small sting, followed by a thin high drone

Mrs Hall Well, go on, then. Or do you want me to find you some more work?

Marvel Unnecessary, madam, I've found a new position for myself. (*He twists and speaks to the air*) Wait for it, wait for it. (*To them, trying to pass it off*) Sorry about that. Touch of lumbago. (*He twists again*) Give me room, will you, give me room. (*To them*) There it goes again. (*To the air—in Bunting's direction*) If you want me, just whistle.

Bunting Oh, I don't think so.

Marvel I wasn't talking to you, I was talking to—my rabbit. (*He clicks his fingers*) Come along, Rowena. Come along. Back to the warren before the contractions start.

He exits, closing the door

Mrs Hall That fellow's got wheels in his head. (*She rises*) And look what he's done to me nice new mat. (*She goes to it, lifts it, dusts it, puts it down again*)

Millie He was talking to himself like that outside. (*She crosses to the bar putting a menu on it that was on top of the piano*)

Bunting (*moving in a little*) Odd chap, altogether.

Wicksteed He certainly seemed interested in these books.

Burdock Yes, tell you what...

As he crosses up to the door, Millie crosses back to the piano stool, and sits. Burdock locks the door

There. Now we're safe from further interruption.

Griffin Ha!

The drone changes to its normal pitch

Burdock (*to Bunting*) There's no need for that, Vicar. If you don't agree, just say so.

Bunting I didn't speak.

Mrs Hall (*moving in to Bunting from his right*) 'Ypnotism. You mark my words. That's why he wore them dark glasses. 'Ypnotize you, soon as look at you.

She shrieks as her arm is twisted behind her, and she is pulled back to the barrel

Griffin Funny stuff, this 'ypnotism, ain't it?

Burdock starts forward

Oh no, you don't!

The bread knife floats up from the barrel and presses to her throat. A sting

Make a move and I'll cut her throat. You've already been kind enough to collect my notebooks, so tie them together…

The knife points at the three men at the bar

You, with the stupid face.

They look at one another

Burdock Must mean you, Wicksteed.

Wicksteed Oh—right. (*He finds a string behind the bar and ties the notebooks into a bundle during the following*)

Griffin As for you, Vicar…

The knife points at him

These are cold days to run around stark, so go and fetch my clothes.

Mrs Hall He can't.

The knife turns back to her

The police took everything away!

Griffin Then we shall have to make do with what we have to hand.

The knife points at the Vicar again

You understand me, Vicar?
Bunting I'm afraid I don't, actually.
Griffin I need clothes——

The knife moves up and down, indicating

—you're wearing some. Get 'em off.
Burdock I say, hang it all, there are ladies present!
Griffin You'd be amazed what you get to see when you're invisible, Squire——

The knife indicates the women

—and if these two are ladies, God help the Empire.

They react, indignant. The knife stabs towards the Vicar

Now do as I say, damn it!

Bunting sits on the stool, L, *hurriedly undressing during the following. The music becomes softer*

Where's Miss Statchell today?
Burdock Fortunately, she just left.
Griffin Pity. We have an affinity. She's certainly a cut above you types.

The knife turns to Millie

You with the thumb in your face—unlock the door.

Giving him a wide berth, she does so, then backs off to the upstage corner of the piano

A Vicar with no trousers... There's a long-running play in this somewhere. (*He whistles*) Marvel! Get in here!

Marvel appears in the doorway

The knife turns to him

Allow me to introduce my loyal subordinate, my Sancho Panza.

Burdock You traitor, Marvel.

Marvel Sorry, sir. He can be very persuasive when he's kicking your head in.

Griffin That's enough! Give him the books and the clothes!

Wicksteed gives Marvel the books. Millie gives him the Vicar's clothes

You see how easy it is with a servant to handle these matters, Marvel? Now run for it, and meet where we agreed. Don't try and give me the slip. I'll find you.

Marvel I don't doubt it, sir.

He exits

Griffin Thank you, Mrs Hall.

She is pushed R, *and the knife floats* C, *menacing them all*

And I warn you all not to follow me, on peril of your lives. And now—goodbye.

The knife is dropped, the door swings, Mrs Hall is released, breaking R, *and the drone stops. Burdock hurries to her*

Burdock Are you all right, Mrs Hall?

Mrs Hall (*rubbing her arm*) Course I'm all right.

Burdock (*crossing to the door*) Then after him!

Bunting But Squire, you heard what he said!

Burdock Burdocks don't sit tight because some see-through blighter tells 'em to! Hurry along, there!

He exits

Bunting (*wailing*) But Squire, my trousers…!

Mrs Hall Bugger your trousers!

She runs out

Wicksteed We must raise hue and cry!

He runs out

Millie Knack the bleeder!

She runs out

Bunting What will my parishioners think?

He runs out

Griffin They'll think you're a fool, Vicar. And seeing how easily I've just fooled you and your friends, who can blame them? Ha!

The stool is pulled to the piano, the lid slammed up

Idiots!

Laughing madly, he crashes up and down the piano, then stops

But what's this I spy? A glass of nutritious milk. Excellent! All this work's made me thirsty.

He tips it and drinks it

Adye enters, carrying the Vicar's clothes

Adye Where's everybody disappearing to? Whole place has gone completely mad.

The clothes are lifted up and examined

Griffin These clothes—where did you find them?

Adye That's another mad thing. Some little tramp just bumped into me and—(*his voice fades as he realizes he is talking to thin air*) dropped them.

Griffin Marvel! You clumsy oaf!

The clothes drag Adye R, *and then* L

Damn it, *I* can't take them! Everybody will see where I'm going!

He kicks Adye's legs from under him, and Adye crashes to the floor

You fool, Marvel! You priceless idiot!

The door bangs shut

Adye (*sitting up dizzily*) Gad, they're right—he *is* invisible. (*He collapses*)

Fast scene-change music. The gauze and blinder fly in, the Light cross-fading to:

SCENE 4

The Chase Begins

A Country Lane. That night

The church bells ring out an alarm pattern: a relentless repeated two-note sound. It is dusk

Wearing coats and scarves, Mrs Hall and Millie hurry on from R, *crossing to* L, *ad-libbing. Also in a coat and scarf, Miss Statchell appears in the arch* R, *behind them*

Miss Statchell Mrs Hall…! Mrs Hall!

They stop and she hurries to them

Is it true? The Invisible Man's been *back*?

Mrs Hall I'll say he's been back. He nearly murdered me.

Millie (*grandly*) And his name's Griffin. We found that out concealed within his notebooks.

Teddy runs on from L

Teddy What's all the bells, Mrs Hall?

Mrs Hall Oh, you report down there, Teddy—(*she point off* L) where you can see the crowd gathering.

Teddy Right you are, Mrs Hall.

He runs off L

Mrs Hall They're getting together everybody they can to form a search party, and the women have got to make the tea.

Millie We're all under the Squire.

Miss Statchell Oh no, we're not! We'll form our *own* search party—(*she puts the pipe in her mouth*) the Ladies Brigade!

Mrs Hall (*dubiously*) Are you sure?

Millie He likes to get his own way, the Squire.

Mrs Hall Last time we crossed him, he took to drinking in the *Hedgehog and Trumpet.*

Miss Statchell Then it's time you stood up for yourself, Mrs Hall, so do as I say. We'll offer our services to Colonel Adye. Where will I find him?

Millie (*pointing* L) That way, miss.

Miss Statchell crosses L *to peer off*

They're splitting up, you see. The Squire to the west——

Mrs Hall As far as Fearenside's farm——

Millie And the Colonel to the east—as far as Dr Kemp's place.

Miss Statchell Kemp? I know that name. No matter. The main thing is, *we* find the Invisible Man first. Those fox-hunting brethren of the Squire's will tear him limb from limb.

Mrs Hall At least we'll be safe in our beds.

Miss Statchell (*putting her arms round their shoulders*) But the blood of an innocent man will be a blot on the fair name of Iping, Mrs Hall, and I know how much that would offend your civic pride—so hurry up. It's going to be a long, hard night.

Casting up her eyes, she exits, L

Mrs Hall (*to Millie*) If I didn't know better, I'd think she was having me on. (*She crosses* L) Bossy cow, ain't she?

She exits L

The blinder flies out

Millie (*following her*) She's one of these here new women, Mrs Hall. You and me are old uns.

She exits

(*Off*) One of us is, anyroad.

She is slapped

(*Off*) Ow!

Scene-change music, and the bells stop. The gauze flies out, towers turn to interior doors, the Light cross-fades to:

Scene 5

The Full Story

Dr Kemp's Study. That night

Kemp, wearing a smoking jacket, enters DR

Kemp (*calling off*) No, I *haven't* read the papers. And you can tell your friends that your respected employer, Dr Kemp, states that invisibility is scientifically impossible. (*He shuts the door and crosses up to the drinks table*) Stupid slut. (*He pours himself a drink*) Invisible Man, indeed. Bad as my old colleague, Griffin. *He* believed in the impossible—(*he crosses* DL) which is why he's dead.

With a crash, the french windows swing open on their own

Then Marvel is propelled into sight and into the room

Marvel Dr Kemp?

Kemp How dare you. This had better be an emergency.

Marvel It will be if he beats me up again. (*To the air*) See? Told you I'd find him. He'll have some clothes. Now does anybody mind if I hop it?

He turns to go, but his arm is twisted up his back

All right, all right, I only asked. (*To Kemp*) It's getting so you can't even open your mouth. (*To the air as he is released*) And I wish you'd stop twisting bits of me. One of 'em'll drop off soon.

Kemp (*carefully*) I think you want Dr Kilbride. *He's* the psychiatrist.

Griffin He's a quack, Kemp. Like you.

Kemp (*staring at Marvel*) How'd you do that? You didn't even open your mouth.

Marvel I'm not allowed to.

He is poked in the eye

Griffin I must say you've done all right for yourself, Gerald. No doubt the fire insurance from the lab helped.

Kemp (*trembling, looking up in the air, crossing to the door* DR) Griffin? Is that you, Griffin? Listen, old man, don't come back to haunt me. It wasn't my fault.

He gasps, throttled

Griffin Shut up! (*As he squeezes*) You'll soon wish I *were* a ghost, Kemp! Ghosts aren't flesh and blood! *They* can't hurt you!

Kemp is released

Kemp (*gasping*) This is nonsense. It's some sort of trick.

Marvel Oh, if only it were. (*He indicates the drinks table*) Is that port I spy? (*He puts the books on the chair,* R, *and pours himself a drink*)

Griffin No trick, Kemp. Look over here on your desk... (*Impatiently*) Over here, in your evening paper...

Kemp crosses to the desk, then reacts back, R, *as pages in the paper turn*

Ah, here I am. Read it to him, Marvel.

Marvel Right. (*He crosses to the desk and bumps into Griffin*) Sorry. (*He reads*) "Village Invaded by Invisible Visitor"... "Special Report by Local Eyewitness, Miss Statchell"... Miss? That can't be right. Women aren't allowed to write for the newspapers.

Griffin This one's different.

Kemp I knew your work was important, but——

Griffin You didn't know what it was. You only knew it was something you could steal to get yourself into the Royal Society. You're a fool, Kemp. Look at what you're working on here. (*Impatiently*) On your desk again.

As Kemp moves to the desk, papers are lifted and a quill pen stands up, slashing, correcting

Wrong—wrong—doubtful—poorly argued—and wrong.

The pen is tossed down

Is it any wonder I went mad when I caught you copying my notebooks?

Marvel Could I go now?

Griffin (*shouting in his ear*) No! Shut up! (*To Kemp*) I'm here to give you one last chance, Gerald. God knows you deserve worse, but I want to put all that behind us. I need your help. Can I trust you?

Kemp Of course.

This is clearly so false that even Marvel notices

Griffin Then fetch me some clothes. This fool—(*he hits Marvel*) lost mine. Anything will do.

Kemp Wait here.

He goes to the door DR, *looks back furtively, and goes out*

Griffin Better shut these doors. Those search parties are getting closer.

Marvel Led by a silly Squire and a daft Colonel? They'll have disappeared up their own backsides by now.

Griffin They can still be here in minutes if they spot us.

The doors close

(*Shivering*) God, it's cold. What's that you're drinking? Give it to me.

The glass flies from Marvel's hand, and he chases it

Marvel Oy, oy! That's mine!
Griffin Then pour me some!

Marvel crosses to the table

Can't you see I'm dying for a drink?
Marvel (*picking up the bottle and a glass*) Where are you?
Griffin (*impatiently*) Over here!

Marvel crosses L, *places the glass in mid air and begins to fill it*

Marvel Say when.
Griffin (*thrusting it back at him*) Damn the man! How long does it take to find a few clothes?

The door DR *is flung open, Griffin's voice moving* DR

Kemp! Where are you? (*He calls down the corridor*) What are you doing out there?

Kemp comes in quickly, a picture of guilt

(*His voice is close*) Where are those clothes?
Kemp Without my housekeeper, I don't seem to be able to lay my hands on anything. There are a few old things I use in the garden hanging up in the hall…
Griffin Anything will do. (*He shoves him aside*) Oh, I'll get them myself. (*To Marvel*) Marvel, keep an eye on him.
Marvel I'll do my best, sir.

He hurries to stand very close to Kemp's back, stares at the back of his neck. Kemp cautiously goes to the door

Kemp (*calling off*) What are we going to do about covering your head, Griffin? I couldn't bear to see just a set of clothes walking about.
Griffin (*off*) We'll think of something.

Kemp shuts the door and turns to find himself nose to nose with Marvel. He moves up, Marvel moves up. He moves down, Marvel moves down. He pushes past him and crosses to L. *Marvel follows*

Kemp What are you doing? Can't you see my brain's rioting? I can't take it all in. For God's sake, this is the scientific discovery of the age.

Marvel I wouldn't know, mate. The only thing I studied at school was truancy.

A sound. Marvel turns to look at the window, Kemp turning to look down stage

What was that?

Marvel hurries up to the windows

Kemp Nothing.

Marvel (*peering out*) Who's that haring off down the road in such a hurry?

Kemp (*mopping his face*) Only the maid. It's her night off. She has a young man in the village. You can trust me.

Marvel I hope so, for your sake. Cross this bloke, and he'll kill you.

Griffin (*off*) Well spoken——

The door bangs open and he is there: an impressive figure in a long coat, boots, black knotted material over his head, handless

—Marvel!

Big long sting. They stare at his head

A lady's stocking, Gerald. In one of the pockets. And you a doctor. Tut tut. Any gloves?

Kemp There's a pair I use in the laboratory—(*he indicates the desk*) second drawer down.

He and Marvel dodge quickly over to R *as Griffin crosses to the desk. Griffin reaches out an empty sleeve, and the drawer handle lifts. The drawer opens. He masks pulling on a glove*

(*Shutting the door*) I still can't believe you're here—in Iping, of all places.

Griffin Why not? (*He turns to them, one white-gloved hand carrying the other glove*) I knew you had a house in the country. (*He uses his invisible* *hand to close the drawer*) It wasn't *my* fault it snowed, and the wretched train got stuck—(*he masks fitting the second glove*)—abandoning me in that ridiculous village. (*He turns, both hands now visible and gloved*) I'd have sought you out earlier, but I needed time to think. It had all happened so fast. Only a few weeks before, I had been working late in my laboratory, and suddenly there it was—the whole principle. I realized immediately what it meant. *I*—a shabby, hemmed-in lecturer from a provincial college could become—*this*! I ask you to imagine my feelings.

Marvel sits at the chair, R

Music underlays

I went outside into the night, and walked for hours. It was like a dream. My whole life floated past, and I realized that for me the world was a desolate place. I had never been part of it, never accepted. So much so that entering the laboratory seemed like a recovery of reality. *There* was my world. *There* were the things I knew and loved. And *there*, Kemp, stood *you*—stealing my notes! The rage I'm always trying to suppress broke out, and I attacked you. The burners went over, the building caught fire…

Kemp You were never found. I thought you were dead.

Griffin It was a close-run thing.

The music stops

What was that?

Kemp What?

Griffin (*opening the door* L) I thought I heard something out there.

Kemp No, no, Griffin, go on, go on.

Griffin (*crossing up to the windows*) I'm sure there's somebody outside.

Kemp (*moving upstage of Marvel*) Only the wind. Keep on.

Griffin There's little more to tell. Except, of course, the greatest story of all. I rebuilt the experiment, and used it on myself, with the results you see. (*He moves downstage*)

Music underlays

A whole night of racking anguish… But as the dawn light rose, I was able to stand before the mirror and see my body turn milky, then glassy, then become a mist and fade until all that was left was—space. It was horrible.

Kemp I can understand that. And yet…

Griffin It was liberating. Yes! I could do as I pleased. Who could catch me? How could I be punished? Never had I felt such confidence! And then——

The music changes

—disillusion. The more I tried, the more I realized what a helpless absurdity an invisible man was in a cold climate in a dirty and crowded city.

Marvel You can have anything you want.

Griffin And enjoy it *how*? In what form? I had become a wrapped-up mystery—a swathed and bandaged caricature of a man! No, what I needed in spite of everything, Kemp, was *you*—a skilled accomplice with a hideout. Somewhere to work from, plan the campaign.

Kemp Campaign?

Griffin If I can't restore my appearance—and so far, I've not found a way—we have to consider the best use to be made of my invisibility.

Kemp And you *have* considered?

Griffin More than that, Kemp. I'm certain. It's in killing.

Big sting in the underlay

Kemp *What?*

Griffin I started off too vague, too haphazard, but now I know, Kemp—now I'm sure. It's killing we must do. Not wanton killing, of course, Gerald. More an organized judicial massacre.

Kemp *Why?*

Griffin *Terror!* They know there's an Invisible Man now, so that Invisible Man must establish a reign of terror! Bring the country to its knees! (*He paces*) There's no end to what we can achieve…! Train smashes…! Munitions exploding…! Leading figures assassinated! Government buildings destroyed! A new kind of warfare from a new kind of man! And the reward? *World domination!*

The music stops

Marvel One minute, it's one thing; one minute, it's another. I can't follow you at all.

Griffin You don't have to, Marvel.

Marvel (*eagerly*) D'you mean that, sir?

Griffin You're a poor tool.

Marvel I am, I am.

Griffin I'm sure I could do better.

Marvel You could, you could.

Griffin But I dare say you'll do.

Marvel Oh, gawd.

Griffin And cheer up. We'll rule the world, you and I, Thomas Marvel.

During the following, Kemp surreptitiously slips up to peer out of the windows

Marvel (*gloomily*) I'm looking forward to it, sir.

Griffin (*to himself*) You, I and my consort—if she'll agree. (*He turns*) And *you*, Kemp—(*he looks for him*) Kemp—(*he sees him at the window, a picture of guilt*) are you with us? Yes or no. There's no in-between.

Kemp Well—if I'm to share—it all sounds very tempting...

Griffin turns away and Kemp is able to register glee at what he sees approaching through the window, before moving casually downstage

Yes, of course I agree. Count me in.

Griffin (*pulling Marvel to his feet, and joining their hands*) Then we'll form a pact, an agreement to support me in the establishment of a new world order, dedicated to the overthrow of poverty and misery—an end to all tyranny. There'll be no dictators when *I* rule the world! (*To both. Harshly*) Whoever breaks this pact dies. Repeat that.

Marvel (*gloomily*)
Kemp (*cheerfully*) } (*together*) Whoever breaks this pact, dies.

Griffin There——

Music

—it's done!

He takes Marvel in his arms

Nothing can stand against us. The world is ours.

Minor waltz. He dances with Marvel

Kemp dances up to the windows, and throws them open to let in Colonel Adye, armed, followed by three caped and moustachioed policemen

Griffin and Marvel dance DR, *Kemp* DL. *Adye moves* DLC, *the policemen stay* UC. *Adye blows a whistle, and the music and dance stop*

Adye Mind if I cut in?

Griffin (*staring; to Kemp, venomously*) So, Kemp. You betrayed me, after all. I should have realized your mind was too puny. (*He goes for his coat buttons*) And now you'll pay.

Adye (*aiming the pistol*) Oh no, you don't. Divest yourself of one article of clothing, and I shall open fire. Besides, there are two hundred policemen and volunteers outside, surrounding the house with their arms linked. You'll never make it.

Brief pause

Griffin Very well. (*He holds out his hands and moves up to the police*) I give in.

Adye (*to a policeman*) Put the cuffs on him, Three-O-Six, there's a good chap.

Griffin suddenly grabs Marvel and uses him as a shield. Music starts

Marvel Here, I thought I was on *your* side! (*To Adye*) Don't shoot, sir! You'll hit *me*!

Adye Does it matter, I'm asking myself.

Griffin throws Marvel at him, and makes a run for the door R. *Adye and Marvel collapse*

Well, get him!

PC 2 Leave it to me, sir!

He grabs Griffin's shoulder

(*To PC 1*) Give us a hand, Syd! He's getting away!

PC 1 grabs Griffin's left hand, holding on. They lunge off and back, PC 2 pulling the long black stocking, which snaps back into his hands

I've pulled this stocking off his head, sir!
PC 1 (*to Griffin*) Come on, you!

He drags the headless Griffin back onstage

Griffin (*headless*) You'll never catch me, you stupid policemen.

He disappears, dragging PC 1 off with him

Adye Look out! He's getting away!

PC 2 runs off stage

Don't let him take anything else off!

PC 2 enters, with the long coat

PC 2 Now I've pulled his coat off, sir!
Adye You fool!

PC 1 puts his head in

PC 1 It's all right, sir, I've still got hold of him!

He disappears

Adye (*to PC 2*) Well, give him a hand!

PC 2 runs off stage

(*To PC 3*) And you—hold on to that evidence!
PC 3 Sir!

He runs out of the windows with the stocking and coat

Adye (*calling off*) Come on, chaps! Move along!

PC 1 appears again

PC 1 Got him, sir.

PC 2 and PC 1 struggle out, fighting with the two white-gloved hands, the rest of Griffin invisible

Here he is, sir.
Adye (*going to them*) Invisible Man, you're under arrest. Do you have anything to say?

The hands heave, and he is kicked in the groin. As he writhes downstage, the two policemen struggle upstage, and then hold up limp white gloves as Griffin breaks free. Kemp is thrust aside with a cry, and the door L *swings open*

PC 1 (*to Adye*) Don't worry, sir, I can see where he's going! (*He runs to the door. He calls off*) You're nicked, mate.

He exits, L

Marvel (*looking down at the writhing Adye; to the audience*) Brings tears to your eyes, don't it?
PC 2 (*to Adye, helping him up*) Are you all right, sir?
Adye Of *course* I'm all right.
Marvel He *likes* writhing on the floor and screaming in agony.
Adye (*to him*) Shut up! (*To PC 2*) Get off! (*To Kemp*) You! (*He indicates* L) Where does that door lead to?
Kemp It's just a cloakroom. There's no way out there.
Adye Then we've got him! (*To PC 2*) And shut those blasted windows!
Marvel Leave it to me, sir! (*He runs up to close them*)
Adye (*calling off* L) How are you doing in there, Three-O-Two?

PC 1 appears at the door

PC 1 (*with one arm off stage*) Piece of cake, sir. I've got the handcuffs on him. (*He comes on fully, to* C, *handcuffs standing out straight from his left wrist*)

PC 2 Good on you, Syd. (*To Adye*) I knew he could do it, sir.
PC 1 (*with smug satisfaction*) He can't get away now.

He is suddenly yanked sideways, then around in a circle. Everybody scatters

Adye Well, keep him under control, man!

PC 1 is dragged to the door R, *and the handcuffs fall limp*

PC 1 (*holding them up*) He's wriggled free, sir!
Kemp For God's sake, get him! If he escapes, we're done for! (*He closes the door,* L)
PC 2 (*going to the door* R) I'll get him, sir.
Adye No, Constable—leave this to me. (*To PC 1*) You—go and get some reinforcements.
PC 1 Sir!

PC 1 runs out, closing the french windows

Adye This time, I'll deal with him myself. (*He goes, pistol ready*) All right, Invisible Man, your last chance. Any more of this, and I fire.

He exits

PC 2 (*to Kemp*) Good job we brought our best men, sir, otherwise this could have been a bit tricky.
Marvel I'm glad you told me. I'd never have guessed.

A yell, off, from Adye

PC 2 (*running to the door*) On me way, sir!
Adye (*off*) No, Constable, stay right where you are!

All freeze, the music stops

He enters with his own pistol at his head, hands raised. He is being pushed up to the windows

Swine got the drop on me. Make the slightest move, and he'll blow my brains out.

Marvel We can't have that. They'll make him Chief Constable.

Behind Adye, one of the doors swings open, but he grapples with the gun, dragging Griffin behind the screen, to reappear with his gun, looking wildly about him

Adye Right, that does it! You'll just have to take your chances! Duck!

All throw themselves flat as he fires six shots indiscriminately around the room. A pause

Marvel D'you think you winged him, sir?
Adye With any luck. Feel about for bits of body and invisible blood. (*He indicates*) And shut those blasted *windows!*
Miss Statchell (*off*) Too late, Colonel!

She runs in through the french windows

He ran from the room before you fired.
Adye How d'you know that?
Miss Statchell He's just burst through my Ladies Brigade.
Kemp *What?*
Miss Statchell We were linking arms with your men, as instructed, but...
Adye He just burst through.
Kemp (*crossing* R) My God, and I led you right to him! He'll kill me for this! (*He closes the door,* R)
Marvel He'll do worse than that—the bloke ain't stable.

Shouts and whistles off stage

There he goes now.
Adye (*to PC* 2) After him!

He runs out, blowing his whistle, followed by PC 2 and Miss Statchell

Kemp Wait for me! Don't leave me alone!

He runs after them, pausing to snatch up the port decanter, and a glass

Marvel (*to the audience*) It's all go, innit?

He runs after them

Fast scene-change music, gauze and blinder fly in, the Light cross-fades to:

SCENE 6

The Chase Continues

Dr Kemp's garden. Same time

Moonlight. An owl hoots

Adye runs on from R

Adye (*calling off behind him*) You cover the front of the house, Constable! I'll be along shortly.

Mrs Hall hobbles on L, *supported by Millie*

(*To Mrs Hall and Millie*) What the devil's going on?
Mrs Hall Her and her Ladies Brigade. He nearly murdered me again.
Adye Which way did he go?
Millie Through the garden.

Adye crosses to stare off L

Mrs Hall He trod all over me feet, then bashed his way through the roses. He'll be picking thorns out of his bum for a week.

Miss Statchell hurries on from R, *to* C, *followed more slowly by Kemp*

Adye Blast. We'll never find him in this light. (*To the women*) How *could* you let him through? I ordered an impenetrable wall of linked human bodies.
Miss Statchell I'm afraid it was *my* fault. I sort of slipped and pulled Mrs Hall out of line.
Millie You didn't slip! You barged into her deliberately on purpose!
Adye (*crossing* R) It would help if we knew in which direction he was

heading. (*He calls off*) You men stop smoking there. The horses don't like it. (*He reloads the pistol*)

Kemp (*pouring port; to Miss Statchell*) We've never met, have we? Why not pop round for a drinkie one evening? I'm awfully good company.

Miss Statchell So's a hamster.

Wicksteed (*off,* L) Colonel!

Millie (*looking off*) It's the Squire and Mr Wicksteed!

Wearing his leather coat and flying helmet, Burdock runs on, followed by Wicksteed. Burdock crosses to Adye, Wicksteed stays L

Marvel enters R, *mopping his brow*

Burdock (*to Adye*) What's all the ruckus? Have you found him?

Adye We had him, but this lady let him go.

Kemp God knows what he's planning now. The man's mad. He wants to take over the government.

Miss Statchell Well, it's time *somebody* did—and being mad's no disqualification.

Marvel (*to Kemp*) It's your fault, Doctor, he's so peeved. He was relying on *you* to help him conquer the world.

Kemp I had no choice: I *had* to betray him.

Marvel Yes, but think what a shock it was. (*To the audience*) I mean, if you can't rely on a man's greed and lust for power, what *can* you rely on?

A smashing of glass and a scream off stage, L

Adye Damn! What's that? (*He runs* L)

Marvel He's breaking people's windows!

Adye Heading towards the village, by the sound of it. (*He is struck by a thought*) Oh, my God!

Burdock What is it?

Wicksteed The Vicar, sir!

Mrs Hall He's called a meeting in the Village Hall!

Millie All the old people who couldn't go out on the search party!

Adye (*running back to Burdock*) We've got to reach them before the Invisible Man does! Hurry along, Squire!

Kemp I'll go back inside and send a telegram to warn the government.

Burdock Good thinking, Doctor.

Kemp exits, R

(*To Adye*) As for you, Colonel—to quote Alfred, Lord Tennyson, "Lead, and I follow!"

Adye Then do so! (*He runs* L) Charge!

He exits, L

Mrs Hall (*following him*) Oh, me eardrums.

She and Millie go out, L

Burdock crosses to follow, but Miss Statchell's voice stops him

Miss Statchell (*to Burdock*) Mathematics, and now poetry. Knowledge isn't the useless stuff you pretend, is it?

Wicksteed He likes to appear stupid, miss. Born to wealth, privilege *and* brains embarrasses him.

Burdock shoves him to the exit L

Burdock Just follow the Colonel.

Wicksteed exits, L

(*To Miss Statchell*) How about you, Miss Statchell?

Miss Statchell I'll round up my Ladies Brigade, and follow as soon as I can.

Burdock Good thinking.

She runs off L *as the blinder flies out*

(*To Marvel*) Marvel, you come with us.

He runs off L

Marvel runs to C

Marvel (*to the audience*) It gets a bit wild now, madam, so I should hold on to your husband. If you haven't got one, hold on to somebody else's. To the Village Hall!

He runs off L

Fast scene-change music, the gauze flies out, the Lighting cross-fades to:

Scene 7

A Warning is Delivered

The Village Hall. Same time

Slight babble of noise from the auditorium, as Bunting moves forward to reassure his parishioners

Behind him is a table covered with a Union Jack, on which are various weapons, a chair either side. Above him, a large sign: "Iping Village Defence Committee. Combating the Invisible Menace"

Bunting (*to the audience*) Please stay calm, everybody! Stay in your seats! (*He calls up to one difficult old lady*) Mrs Humpage! (*To the rest*) There's safety in numbers, and he only appears to be breaking a few windows.
Marvel (*off*) He's doing worse than that, Vicar!

Musical ping

Marvel pops on, L

The Lights check quickly except for follow spots on Bunting and Marvel

He's in a right tantrum! He's just cut all the telephone wires!
Bunting What?
Marvel He's thrown old Mrs Moffatt into the pond, and terrorized Miss Batchett in her bath!
Bunting Good Lord!
Marvel He's set fire to the police station, turned over everybody's

dustbins, and kicked a cat over a haystack. But don't worry—I'm with a party on its way here to rescue you.

A ping, and Lighting is restored

Marvel disappears

Bunting Thank you very much. The point is—(*he does a take and stares at the space just occupied by Marvel*) the point is, he hasn't actually *hurt* anybody yet—(*he moves to the table*) and if we use these weapons I've gathered, then the viper that little Iping took to her bosom—(*he picks up a rounders bat*) and who repaid our trust with wholesale mayhem—(*he smashes it down on to the table, enjoying it*) shall be destroyed! (*He tosses it down*) All I need are some volunteers.

The Lights flicker and dim to a red glow. A big sting

Who turned the lights out?
Griffin Who do you think, *Vicar*?

The chair, R, *is kicked over. Bunting stares at it, backing to the table*

Bunting (*in a small voice*) Volunteers? Do I have any volunteers?
Griffin Yes, Vicar, *here's* one——

Behind Bunting, one of the weapons—a cane carpet-beater—floats into the air

—volunteering to give you a good hiding!

Bunting yells, breaking downstage, away from the table, as the carpet beater belabours him. It is tossed aside

Nobody calls me names any more—*nobody*!

The long scarf wraps itself around Bunting's throat and begins to strangle him

Marvel (*off*) It's all right, Vicar, we're on our way!

He runs on, and Bunting is released, gasping

(*To the audience*) See? Just in the nick of time.

Adye runs on and goes to Bunting

Adye Are you all right, Padre?

Bunting gurgles, gasps and points at his throat

Good.

Burdock hurries on to C, *followed by Mrs Hall and Millie, who stay* R, *to Marvel's right*

He must still be on stage.
Burdock (*in a low voice*) Feel around, everybody. (*He indicates* L) Over there, Wicksteed.

They feel about. Wicksteed crosses to L

Adye You too, Marvel.
Marvel I can't.
Adye Why not?
Marvel He's standing on my foot.

A sting. Women scream and react back. Adye runs to C

Adye (*aiming*) Duck, man! Duck!
Griffin No, Colonel—*you* duck!

He wrestles with Adye's gun

Burdock (*running* R, *spreading his arms*) Behind me, ladies!

Adye drops the gun behind the table, retires L, *wringing his hand*

Griffin It's time we dealt with you small-minded peasants once and for all.

The gun floats up, aimed at Adye, who snatches up a stick from the table and slashes at it, above and below. Griffin laughs. Defeated, Adye drops the stick, backs off, hands raised

You first, Colonel. This time, it's curtains.

Adye throws himself flat. The gun fires at him, blowing Wicksteed's hat off. Burdock jumps forward and rabbit-punches Griffin

Damn!

The gun is dropped. Burdock pushes Griffin L, *and snatches up the gun*

Burdock Now we've got him! Don't let him off the stage! Block all the exits!

Stings as they do so, arms spread wide: Wicksteed blocks the steps to the auditorium L; *Adye the arch* L; *Bunting the exit above the arch* L; *Burdock the split in the curtains* C; *Millie the exit above the arch* R; *Mrs Hall the arch* R; *and Marvel the steps leading into the auditorium* R

Marvel Don't worry, sir—he won't get past me!

He is thrust aside, and feet are heard banging down the steps into the auditorium. The drone stops

Adye (*running to* C) Oh my God, he's got into the auditorium!
Burdock (*joining him; to the audience*) Don't panic, everybody. Keep calm. There's absolutely no cause for alarm.

Fiona gives a piercing scream rear of the stalls

NB: Use should be made of any parties in the auditorium. Larry is the actor playing Kemp; Fiona, the understudy or from stage management

Marvel There he goes!
Adye After him! (*He runs*) Bolt all the doors!

All the men rush into the auditorium, using both sets of steps

Burdock (*running*) Don't let him out the building!

Mrs Hall and Millie run L

Mrs Hall (*calling after them*) Do you want the women to make the tea?

Miss Statchell appears, R

Miss Statchell (*calling off*) I'll be with you in a minute, ladies. (*She hurries across to Mrs Hall and Millie*) What is it? What's going on?
Millie It's the Invisible Man!
Mrs Hall He's running riot round the audience!

Fiona gives another piercing scream

See what I mean?
Larry (*in the dress circle*) He's up here!
Bunting (*in the rear stalls*) No, he's not, he's down here!
Mrs Hall (*pointing up*) No, he isn't, Vicar, he's up there!
Millie (*pointing down*) No, he isn't, Mrs Hall, he's down there!
Mrs Hall (*to Miss Statchell*) Can *you* see him?
Miss Statchell Nobody can *see* him, Mrs Hall—only the effect he has on other people.

Larry yells in the dress circle

Like that, for example.
Millie Well, don't you think we ought to help?
Miss Statchell Why? He's only having fun.

Adye runs onstage

Adye (*calling out*) Padre, you take the top, I'll take the middle, you two take the stalls! (*To the ladies*) And *keep* calm!

He runs off

Marvel runs on

Marvel (*to the women*) Don't *panic*!

He runs into the auditorium

Fiona (*in a box*) Ah! Something touched me!
Larry That's no Invisible Man, darling.
Marvel Careful where you put your hands! He's got nothing on!

Burdock runs onstage

Burdock (*calling up*) Any sign, Vicar? Who've you got up there?
Bunting (*in the gallery*) Just a few elderly villagers, sir. The Old Ladies Knitting Club. Oh, and Mrs Humpage.
Burdock Colonel?
Adye (*in the dress circle*) A bunch of bed-ridden bell-ringers, and the Over Eighties Church Choir, by the look of it, sir.
Burdock Marvel? Who have you got down here?
Marvel (*in the stalls*) Some elderly muck-spreaders, a rather rowdy party of pissed ploughmen, and—(*a bit surprised*) a Jersey cow.

"Moo" from the rear of the stalls. Marvel chases it

Go on, shoo, shoo!
Wicksteed A fairly typical audience for this place, I'm afraid.
Burdock But what about the Invisible Man? Any sign of him?
All (*severally*) No... Not here... Not a sign.
Marvel There's a woman down here says she's been married to one for the last fifteen years.
Burdock Never mind about that. You'd better come back onstage. We'll watch and listen from here.

During the following, Wicksteed, Marvel, Adye and Bunting return on stage: Marvel and Wicksteed R, *Adye and Burdock* RC, *Bunting with Millie and Mrs Hall*

Miss Statchell (*to the women*) Unbelievable. And these are all men—members of the so-called dominant sex.
Millie My mum says they're only good for one thing.
Mrs Hall Yes, and once you've spent it, what have you got left?
Burdock Ladies, please! Miss Statchell, this is *serious*!

A thin drone. All peer out front

(*To Adye. Softly*) Anything?

Adye Not a sign of life.

Mrs Hall (*peering*) No...

Adye Quiet as the grave.

Marvel whimpers. Adye, Burdock, and Wicksteed run to him

All What is it? What is it?

Marvel points at the red curtain. It is moving. All turn, look, yell, and shush one another. Adye and Burdock stalk the movement, and grab a shape through the curtain

Wicksteed Keep the material round him! It's making him visible!

A white-gloved hand clutches Burdock's neck, then a furious Dr Kemp appears, wearing a hat and coat

Kemp What are you doing, you stupid nincompoops?

Burdock (*releasing him*) Dr Kemp!

Adye We thought you were at home, sir.

They all move DC

Kemp I sent a telegram, then decided I'd be safer with you lot. Obviously I'm mistaken.

Griffin (*his voice ringing down from the gallery*) It makes no difference, you're dead anyway, Gerald!

Big sting. Music underlays all that follows. Adye aims his gun, searching for a target

No, Colonel—not if you wish to learn what I have to say.

Burdock (*pushing down Adye's gun*) Why *are* you here?

Griffin To deliver a warning! You may send *another* telegram, Colonel—and in it you may inform your superiors that the terror I promised begins *now*. In one week, I'll bring this class-ridden society to its knees. And *you*, Kemp, a typical product—shall have the privilege of ringing down the curtain. For that is how the terror shall end—with your traitor's death. In one week's time, Kemp—at *noon precisely*—wherever you hide—the revenger of all ills shall seek you out.

Kemp (*on his knees; to Adye*) This is your responsibility, Colonel! I demand protective custody.

Adye We'll look after you, sir. Please be quiet.

Miss Statchell (*moving* LC) Is all this necessary? If you have grievances, why not come down and address them here?

Griffin (*mockingly*) Throw myself on their mercy?

Miss Statchell I'll help all I can.

The music softens

Griffin I believe that. And my offer holds. There is still room for a woman by my side. And who I love shall have a world to share.

Millie She's in league with him!

Mrs Hall (*to Miss Statchell*) You and your new-fangled ideas!

Bunting Remember Jezebel, Miss Statchell.

Griffin Enough! You have heard my demands! In one week's time, Kemp will be dead, and a reign of terror will have delivered the country into my domain. When next we meet, it shall be to bow down to *me*—Invisible Man the First—Ruler of the World!

Auditorium door bangs, and the music stops. A pause

Adye Do you think he meant all that?

Marvel Oh, yes. He's off his rocker, and he thinks he's God. He ought to be in politics, really.

Burdock (*to Miss Statchell; quietly*) We'd better get you out of Iping. That transparent Casanova's put you in a bit of a spot with—(*he indicates a tight-lipped group of villagers*) the local Watch Committee.

The villagers look away

Miss Statchell (*looking at them*) Well, now that I've decided to stay——

They turn to look at her, drawing in their breaths

—they may as well get used to it.

They exhale, furious

(*To Burdock. Coyly*) And it was good of you to care.

He nods casually and turns away, clenching his fists in triumph

Wicksteed (*to Adye*) Better brace yourself, Colonel.
Marvel (*to the others*) And you lot. We're really in for it now. This is going to be a very interesting week.

An explosion

Adye Good God, what's that? Don't tell me he's started already!

As he goes to run off R, *the Lights fade fast to Black-out*

The long whistle of an approaching train, during which the gauze and the blinder fly in, the towers turn to arches. The huge smash of a crashing train. At the end of it, a chord, and the Light builds on:

Scene 8

The Reign of Terror

Everywhere. The following week

During the following, Bunting is Newsboy 1 and 6, Adye is Newsboy 2, Millie is Newsboy 3, Kemp is Newsboy 4, Mrs Hall is Newsboy 5

Tight spot L *into which walks Newsboy 1, carrying a paper in one hand and a big placard in the other, which simply says "Monday!". Throughout this scene, in the background, a sound montage of mayhem: shots, explosions, screams, crackling flames, etc.*

Newsboy 1 Read All About It! Read All About It! Massive Train Crash! Hundreds Killed! Signalman Swears Lever Moved On Its Own! Read All About It!

Fast cross-fade to tight spot R

Newsboy 2 with a placard: "Tuesday!"

A chord

Newsboy 2 Extra! Extra! Huge Explosion Rocks Capital! Naked Flame Seen Floating Towards Kennington Gas Holder Minutes Before Blast!

The blinder flies out

New Fire Of London Raging! Invisible Man Suspected! Extra!

Fast cross-fade to tight spot L. *Flames flicker on the gauze*

Newsboy 3 with a placard: "Wednesday!"

A chord

Newsboy 3 Star News Standard! Star News Standard! Runaway Steam-roller Flattens Royal Garden Party! Rat Poison In Reservoir Wipes Out Windsor! Empty Suit Of Armour Assassinates Archbishop! State Of Emergency Declared! All Police Leave Cancelled! Star News Standard!

Fast cross-fade to tight spot R

Through the flames and the gauze, the Invisible Man is seen, suspended in space

Newsboy 4 with a placard: "Thursday!"

A chord

Newsboy 4 Late Night Final! Late Night Final! Tramlines Connected To National Grid! Millions Electrocuted! Acid Poured Into House Of Lords' Bath-Water! Many Dissolved! Big Invisible Man Hunt! Late Night Final!

Fast cross-fade to tight spot L. *The Invisible Man plays with his hands, and a globe of the world floats up at his command*

Newsboy 5 with a placard: "Friday!"

A chord

Newsboy 5 Special Edition! Special Edition! Lions Released from London Zoo Eat War Cabinet! Sewage Farm Inundates Slough! No Damage Reported! Bomb Demolishes Northern Line! Timetable Not Affected! Special Edition!

Fast cross-fade to tight spot R. *The globe flies about the Invisible Man's head, controlled by him, floating in space*

Newsboy 6 with a placard: "Saturday!"

A chord

Newsboy 6 Read All About It! Read All About It! All Troops Mobilized! Fleet Leaves Scapa Flow For Albert Dock! Nelson's Column Toppled! Houses Of Parliament Razed! Buckingham Palace Destroyed! Queen Mum In Ashes! Tottenham Get Two In Extra Time! Government In Disarray! General Strike! Hospitals Overflowing! All Trains Cancelled! Read All About It!

He exits, R

His Light, the flames and the Invisible Man, the mayhem, fade out. The Light builds to full downstage

Marvel enters from L

The blinder flies in

Marvel What was there to say? England was on her knees. What was left of the Cabinet had no choice but to consider surrender—an act which they knew would hand over the reins of government to the Invisible Man. It all seemed over. Except... For one last desperate throw in the tiniest corner of the Empire——

The blinder flies out

—that insignificant parcel of England which had seen the beginnings of the drama all those months ago—the little village of Iping.

Village music

The Light bleeds through the gauze, and we see Kemp pacing in the prison cell

Here, Dr Kemp had been given his protective custody, and it was here—*at noon precisely*—the Invisible Man had sworn to kill him. Was it possible to set a trap? To confront him here, and defeat him? Certainly, some brave souls thought so.

Music ends on a minor sting. The gauze flies out, towers turn to cell door R, *wall* L, *and Lighting fills from the front to:*

Scene 9

Plot and Counter-Plot

The police station. One week later, noon

Marvel enters the prison cell and sits on the chair, L

Kemp (*trembling*) Where is everybody? It's nearly noon!
Marvel Give 'em a chance. They're still scraping up *yesterday's* casualties.

Kemp climbs the bench to the window

Adye enters

Adye (*calling off*) How should I know the password? I'm the bloke in charge. (*To others*) Hurry along there, chaps. (*He crosses to* C) Bloody Army. Don't know their betters.

Miss Statchell enters and crosses LC, *followed by Burdock who moves* UC, *and Wicksteed, who puts a bag down* UR

Kemp Lock that door, for God's sake!

He jumps down, crosses to it as Adye locks it

Adye (*soothing*) Don't worry, sir. This time, there are *three* hundred policemen outside—all handcuffed together. (*He crosses to Miss Statchell*) No "pulling anybody out of line" this time. (*He climbs on to the bench*)

Miss Statchell I still say we should go out and *talk* to Griffin.

Burdock It's a little late for that.

Marvel Anyway, you *can't* talk to him. All he does is hit you.

Adye tosses the key out of the barred window

Wicksteed Colonel, what are you *doing*?

Adye I've locked the door, and that was the only key. (*He jumps down*) If he wants to get in here, he'll have to force his way in, and while he's doing so the Army will nab him. (*He crosses to Kemp*) D'you know, the Imperial General Staff are running the show themselves—just outside the village.

Miss Statchell (*to Marvel*) Or to put it another way, just out of range.

Kemp crosses to C, *trembling*

Burdock (*to Wicksteed*) How long till noon, Wicksteed?

Wicksteed (*checking his watch*) Fifteen seconds, sir.

Burdock (*producing a pistol*) Then, gentlemen, cock your pieces.

Burdock, Adye and Wicksteed form a huddle, R

Marvel I beg your pardon?

They cock their pistols

Oh. (*To the audience*) I knew it was something *I* couldn't do.

He moves the chair DL *and hides behind it*

Burdock (*to Miss Statchell*) I promise not to fire unless absolutely necessary. (*To Adye*) The door, Colonel. (*To Wicksteed*) By the table, Wicksteed. (*To Miss Statchell*) Miss Statchell, with me, please.

He takes his own place left of the bed, covering the window. Wicksteed covers it from R. *Adye covers the door. Kemp cowers* C

Right. Here we go, then.

Brief pause, then the church clock starts to strike twelve. Kemp groans and falls to his knees, C

Kemp That's it! That's it! He's coming!
Burdock Get a grip, man. You're letting the side down.
Marvel It's cowardice, sir. You see a lot of it in the middle-classes.
Kemp How dare you address me in that fashion, you mere tramp? I'm a doctor! (*He shows him*) Look—here's my silver fob-watch!
Miss Statchell Oh, be quiet, you silly little man!
Wicksteed I'll restrain him if he gets out of hand, miss.
Marvel Don't tell me you used to be a ju-jitsu expert, as well.
Burdock Not for long. Interfered with his tap-dancing.

The last chime dies. Pause. They relax

Adye (*displeased, moving to* C) That's that, then. He's not coming. In which case——

A bright flash of Light and a huge explosion. All are thrown to the floor, except Burdock who is thrown on top of Miss Statchell on the bed

What the devil was that? (*He jumps to his feet, and tugs at the door*) Oh, blast! The door's locked! (*He runs to the bed and glares at Burdock and Miss Statchell*) Excuse *me*.

Burdock is tipped on the floor, and Miss Statchell rises to UL, *flustered. Adye jumps up onto the bed, to the window*

(*Calling*) You, there! What the hell's going on?

Army-style gibberish, off

All of them?

Army-style gibberish, off

Tell the Brigadier I'll be out as soon as I can.

Army-style gibberish, off. He turns to them, a bit shame-faced

The Imperial General Staff...

Burdock Blown up?

Adye Pretty much.

Kemp (*rising and crossing to the door, overcome*) Then he wasn't after me, after all!

Miss Statchell (*moving to* C) Of course not. It was just a trick.

Adye steps off the bed and moves DC

Marvel (*to the audience*) And they all fell for it.

Adye The last centre of organized resistance—*gone*! Now we'll *have* to capitulate.

Burdock (*running to the door*) Not yet, we don't!

Miss Statchell Well, you can't get out. This bright spark's thrown the key away.

Adye (*to Burdock*) If I may be allowed, sir... (*He glances at the lock*) Oh yes, a simple double-lever Bramah with patent deadlock. Nothing to a man with my talent for picking locks. (*He blows the lock off the door with one shot from his pistol*)

The door springs open and he runs out

(*Off*) Right, you men! Form fours! Mount your horses! Charge towards that smoke!

Burdock (*at the door*) He tries his best, but we'd better get out there and take charge, Wicksteed. Got the gubbins?

Wicksteed Sir. (*He hurries* UR *and picks up the bag*)

Burdock How about you, Marvel? Game for the fray?

Marvel Game for anything, sir. I owe him a few knocks. (*He detaches his stick from his bundle*)

Burdock (*to Miss Statchell*) You stay in here. It might get dangerous.

Miss Statchell Keep telling me what to do, and you can *catch* that boat to India.

Burdock I haven't actually bought a ticket yet, old girl.

Miss Statchell Then don't. *I'll* tell you when you've been rejected.

Pause as he moons over her, Wicksteed looking backwards and forwards between them, then tapping him on the shoulder

Wicksteed The Invisible Man, sir.

He still gets no response

The End of Civilization as We Know It.

Burdock (*recovering*) Yes, right! (*He gestures*) Lead on, Wicksteed!

Wicksteed I'm right behind you, sir.

Burdock Follow us, Marvel!

He and Wicksteed run out

Marvel (*waving his stick*) The worm has turned!

He runs out

Miss Statchell climbs on to the bench to look out of the window as we hear shouted orders, revving engines, driving off. Kemp moves slowly to her, looking her up and down

Kemp What can you see?

Miss Statchell There's a big cloud of smoke. They're all pulling out and heading towards it.

Kemp He'll outwit them. He always was a clever little swine.

Miss Statchell It's turning the sky black. It's eerie—as if a storm were brewing.

Kemp (*touching her*) Let me help you down.

Miss Statchell I've had quite enough help for one day, thank you.

She steps down, stumbles, and he holds her

Let go of me.

Kemp (*pulling her closer*) Women always say the opposite of what they really want.

Miss Statchell (*melting*) You're right. I'm so attracted to you.

She stamps on his instep, and he yells, hopping

Not very ladylike, but if I *were* one you wouldn't have treated me this way.

She crosses to the door. It slams in her face. A sting and sinister drone

Griffin I said I'd be back in a week, Gerald.
Kemp (*terrified*) You said *noon*! You promised *noon*!
Griffin (*mimicking him*) I was *lying*!
Kemp (*flailing at the air*) No! No! Leave me alone! I'm a doctor! I've got my life in front of me! Get off, and leave me alone! (*He cowers* DL, *blubbering*)
Griffin What do *you* think, Mrs Statchell?

Kemp's tie stands up as Griffin yanks him to his knees

Shall I kill him?
Miss Statchell Stop tormenting him. It's monstrous. Leave him alone.

Kemp is released

Griffin Soft, like all your sex. I offer you power, and you give me pity. For what? This race of pathetic sub-beings?

Kemp is kicked

You mustn't turn away... We're the same, you and I.

Her hand is taken, she is turned and led to the bench

But I can't manage alone. You have experience in fighting for your beliefs. I have none.

He sits her down

Miss Statchell There are plenty like me.

The mattress depresses as he sits beside her, and takes her hand

Griffin They won't *be* you, Miss Statchell. Why do you think I returned? To kill *that*?

Kemp moans

I knew this was a trap, and yet I risked everything to come here—my liberty, my life. Support me, and I'll worship you, I'll give you whatever you desire.

The music softens

Miss Statchell There's nothing I can do. I supported you when I thought you were helpless and persecuted. But now, you've just got to be stopped. You've become a monster.

Pause

Griffin I'm alone, then?
Miss Statchell (*gently*) Haven't you always been?
Griffin Yes. My great sorrow, but also my strength. I see it clearly now. I can't have you *and* the world. So I must rid myself of the distraction.

The hand is dropped and the mattress rises

You came too close, Miss Statchell. You made me vulnerable. So now I shall have to kill you.

A sting and heavier music. She rises, staring about her. She moves to the door, but is taken by the throat and forced to her knees

Miss Statchell (*choking*) Help me, Kemp! Help me! He's right here!

Kemp rises, then with a cry of terror, runs from the cell

Griffin (*panting*) He'll pay for deserting you. I shall pursue him, and deal with him—*thus*.

She gasps, on her back now

Then all will be over, and the world will be mine.

Burdock runs in

Burdock Oh no, it won't! Release her, you blaggard!

She is released and Burdock is hit in the stomach. He staggers, facing up stage. The following happens very fast, Burdock completely helpless, the music a high-pitched sinister wail: he is hit three times in the face, he twists to the front, his head is twisted in a lock, and he is thrown on to the floor. He is kicked three times. Miss Statchell throws herself over Burdock

Miss Statchell Stop it! Stop it! Leave us alone!

A pause, Griffin panting

Griffin So that's it. Well, you can keep him, then, if that's all you want. You're not *worth* killing, either of you...! (*His voice gets stronger*) But there's one traitor who *won't* escape! (*His voice moves to the door, fading*) I'm coming for you, Kemp! *And* that damned village! They'll all *die*...!

The door slams shut. Miss Statchell and Burdock struggle to their knees, gasping

Burdock
Miss Statchell } (*together*) Are you all right? Don't worry about me. We've got to warn the villagers.

They rise. Miss Statchell runs to the door

Burdock Wait! (*He jumps on to the bench. He calls out the window*) Wicksteed!
Wicksteed (*off*) Sir!
Burdock Find Colonel Adye, and get those men back! Tell the villagers to take cover! He's *here*!

Black-out. The gauze and blinder fly in. The Lights build on:

Scene 10

The Final Reckoning

The Village Green. Same time

Grey clouds scud across the gauze. The sound of the bells ringing an alarm as before

Mrs Hall (*off*) The Invisible Man's here!
Fearenside (*off*) Bolt your doors!
Bunting (*off*) Close your windows!
Mrs Hall (*off*) Stay inside!

The blinder flies out

Fearenside (*off*) The Invisible Man—he's a-comin'!

Bleed through the gauze to the Village Green

We see the panic-stricken Kemp run on from UL, *and the gauze flies out*

The Lighting is stormy, clouds creating smoke as they pass across the set. Kemp runs to bang at the pub door

Kemp Let me in! He's after me!
Mrs Hall (*off*) Well, I hope he gets you.

Kemp runs across and bangs at the wood shed

Kemp For God's sake, let me in! I'm a doctor!
Fearenside (*off*) Get away, you bastard! I'm not opening this door for nobody!

Kemp runs back to C. *As he does so, the bells stop. He reacts, peering wildly about him. He sees a couple of crates outside the pub, with a hammer lying on top, and he snatches it up*

Kemp (*waving it, peering about; quietly*) All right, Griffin, where are you? I'm ready for you.

Griffin Aha!

The hammer flies from Kemp's hand, and he is thrown to the ground. First one leg, then the other, then one arm, then the other, are twisted back. He gasps, helpless, and looks slightly comic as well as caught in what is a type of Boston Crab, his back liable to break

A pause, then, very slowly, the villagers appear, one at a time. First, Fearenside from the woodshed, carrying a spade, then Bunting from UL, *carrying an ice-axe, then Marvel from* UR, *carrying his stick, then Mrs Hall and Millie from the pub; Mrs Hall carrying a broom, Millie a rolling-pin. They slowly form a circle around Kemp, Millie* DC

Fearenside (*whispering*) He's there...
Mrs Hall (*whispering*) Right there in front of us...
Marvel (*whispering*) You can almost see him...
Millie (*whispering*) The fiend without a face...
Fearenside Get the bastard.
Bunting (*shouting*) Vengeance is mine, saith the Lord!

They aim blows in the space above Kemp once, twice. On the second blow, Kemp is released, and rolls aside, DR. *The third blow only hits the ground*

Burdock, Miss Statchell and Wicksteed run on from UR

As they do so, Marvel is knocked aside, followed by Wicksteed

Wicksteed (*pointing off* UR) I felt him brush past me, sir!

During the following, Burdock moves DL, *followed by Miss Statchell and Wicksteed. The villagers rush* UR, *waving their weapons*

Burdock There's no escape that way! We found some of the Army chaps!
Bunting Back you come, Griffin! We're waiting for you!

Ad-lib shouts from the villagers

Wicksteed (*to Burdock*) I don't like the look of this mob, sir. They want blood.
Miss Statchell With this bunch, are you surprised by that?

Bunting is knocked aside, followed in quick succession by Millie and Burdock

Millie He's back! I felt him!

They stare DL

Kemp (*to Fearenside*) Give me that spade! (*He snatches it and crosses* DL)

Burdock is knocked aside, followed by Mrs Hall

Mrs Hall (*pointing off* UL) That way!

Kemp hurries UC

Fearenside He won't get through there, neither! He's trapped!
Burdock (*crossing* R) Then he'll have to come back here! Wicksteed, do your stuff!
Wicksteed (*joining him*) Right, sir!

Kemp joins them as Wicksteed kneels, takes a grenade from the bag, pulls the pin out with his teeth, and throws it off UL. *A soft explosion, and smoke pours out*

Burdock Little idea of mine. Smoke grenades. He sets one foot in there, and we'll see the movement.

A sudden sharp swirl in the smoke. Music

Kemp I saw it! He's *in* there! (*He runs up to the smoke and cuts savagely with the edge of the spade*)

A terrible cry from Griffin

I hit him! I hit him!
Bunting Well, hit him again!

The villagers cheer

Marvel Kill the monster!

Kemp cuts again. Another terrible cry. Kemp holds the spade in Griffin's body

Griffin Mercy… Mercy…

Kemp pulls the spade free, and lifts it high to administer the coup de grâce. *Miss Statchell runs to him to hold him*

Miss Statchell Stop it! We're not animals, for God's sake!
Kemp Get off me, you bitch!

He throws her L, *and Burdock steps in, grappling with him. They strain for the spade, but Burdock pulls it free, smashing Kemp in the face with it. He collapses and crawls* DL. *Burdock looks at Miss Statchell, who seems to melt a little. Burdock feels rather fine for a moment, then turns* UL, *reacting as he steps on Griffin's leg. Griffin groans. Burdock hands the spade to Miss Statchell, moving round to look down at the space*

Miss Statchell (*to the villagers*) Well, I hope you're all pleased with yourselves.

The villagers shift and look at one another. Mrs Hall gives her broom to Millie, kneels and feels the space

Mrs Hall There's a wound in his side… Ugh… (*She holds up her hand*) Blood.
Miss Statchell (*staring at it*) We can *see* it.
Burdock Sit him up. He'll be easier to look after if we know where he is.

During the following, Wicksteed pulls the table aside and Fearenside and Bunting move the chair to C, *Millie moving* DC, *Mrs Hall* UR

Millie, get something to cover him with. Somebody fetch one of those Army nurses.
Fearenside Leave it to me, Squire.

Millie goes into the pub

Fearenside runs off UR

Straining, Bunting, R, *and Burdock,* L, *heave up the groaning Griffin, dropping him into the chair, which shifts a little under his weight. Burdock rejoins Miss Statchell,* L

Bunting (*moving* UL) I must say I feel a little…
Marvel Ssh! (*He moves to the chair,* R)

A whispering

(*To Miss Statchell*) He wants you to hold his hand, miss.

She looks at Burdock, goes to the chair, finds the hand and holds it

Griffin We could have done wonderful things… But you did make me—vulnerable.

The music stops. He sighs, dead. She lays the hand in his lap, and returns to Burdock

Millie enters from the pub, carrying a blanket

She and Mrs Hall shake it out, and cover the chair with it, the shape of Griffin's body immediately forming beneath it

Adye (*off*) You men stay back!

He runs on from UR

Mrs Hall puts an arm round Millie, right of the chair

(*Crossing left of the chair*) I'm keeping the area cordoned off until we're absolutely sure! (*He points his pistol at Griffin's head*) Good Lord! Is that *him*?
Marvel Too late, I'm afraid.
Burdock He can't hurt us any more.

Kemp sniggers. He crosses to C, *laughs at the dead Griffin, turns, and goes into the pub*

Adye jumps down, glaring off after him

Adye Blast! (*He calls off*) Where's that Army nurse? Send her over here.

The nurse hurries on from UR, *meeting Adye above the chair,* L

Don't be afraid, my dear. Go to the Squire.

She crosses to Burdock

Burdock (*to her*) He's under the blanket.

She turns to look

Prepare yourself for a strange sight. He's—completely invisible.

Music. She hands him the bag, crosses to the chair, lifts the blanket, looks beneath it, looks at Burdock, and throws back the blanket. The dead Griffin sits there. All move in

Miss Statchell He's become visible in death.
Mrs Hall Funny. He looks just the same as anybody else.

Music builds. The gauze and blinder fly slowly in, Light cross-fading to downstage area, leaving Marvel. The music stops

Marvel And so ended the strange and evil experiment of the Invisible Man. For those of us who suffered his extraordinary irascibility, it was hard to feel sympathy. We were bound to be enemies. We were too different. And yet, what he must have endured! All his life to go unnoticed, and then to make this great discovery—which made him even *more* unnoticeable. Is it any wonder he went a little mad? As for me—(*he looks about him carefully, crosses to the shed, opens the door, and takes out the bundle of notebooks*) I managed to hold on to *these*. His notebooks. (*He opens them and reads them in anticipation*) "X. Little two up in the air." (*He peers closer, but that is what it says*) "Y. Little three up in the air. Squiggly higgledy-piggledy fiddle-dee-dee, fiddle-dee-dee..."

As he shakes his head mournfully, the blinder flies out

Will anybody ever be able to understand them? I doubt it. But——

Drum-roll. The Light bleeds through gauze

—they're full of secrets, all the same—wonderful secrets. And one day—who knows?

The gauze flies out. In comes a large box with steps up to it, marked "The Amazing Mr Marvel"

Posed R, *are Mrs Hall, Millie and Miss Statchell.* L *and above, are Burdock, Jaffers (in a neck brace), Adye and Wicksteed*

Music. Under Mrs Hall's direction, Millie and Miss Statchell dance across and relieve Marvel of his stick and books

They take them off into the pub

Rubbing his hands, Marvel goes to follow them, but Mrs Hall grabs him and leads him up to the steps, where Adye presents a knee for him to use to climb into the box. Bunting opens the lid for him

(*Waving to the audience*) Bye-bye!

Millie, Mrs Hall, and Miss Statchell dance R

Marvel disappears

Bunting closes the lid. Chains are lowered, and attached

Jaffers (*gesturing to fly-men*) Hup!

The box is lifted a few inches

Adye and Bunting wheel the steps off UL

Burdock moves DC, *and gestures to the band to cut the music, which they do. He turns upstage, and gestures*

Burdock Hup!

The box flies out fully. Drum-roll. Burdock turns to the front again, and produces a gun. He presents it to all parts of the house, each movement punctuated with a crescendo in the roll. He turns back up stage and kneels

Are you ready?
Marvel (*in the box; muffled*) Ready.

Burdock fires. The sides of the box fall down. It is empty. Fanfare

All (*pointing to the box*) Ooh!

They turn and point to an auditorium box where the Light picks out Marvel, now dressed in a silver cloak and top hat. Fanfare

All (*pointing at Marvel*) Ooh!
Marvel (*to the audience*) Maybe there's something in it, after all!

Music. They sing, moving to form a line down stage

Marvel exits, and the Light on him disappears

Song 3: 1904! (Reprise)

All Nineteen-o-four!
That's when it began
The year when we encountered the Invisible Man
Women He came from out of nowhere and he caused a lot of fuss
Men But we are very British and he didn't bother us
All Nineteen-o-four!
That's when it began
The year when we confronted the Invisible Man
Women We never got to speak to him or know him properly

Marvel enters and joins the line, C

Marvel 'Cos like an honest copper he was very hard to see

All Nineteen-o-four!
That's when it began
The year when we defeated the Invisible Man

Men Though he was just a bloke like us who merely said as how

Griffin enters and joins the line, C, *wearing a hat and glasses*

Griffin He ought to run the world as well as them that does it now
The rest He ought to run the world as well as them that does it now
Group 1 The incredible
Group 2 Incomparable
Group 3 Indisputably
All Invisible Man!

Griffin takes his hat and glasses off

CURTAIN

FURNITURE AND PROPERTY LIST

Further dressing may be added at the director's discretion

ACT I

Scene 1

On stage: Union Jacks
French and Japanese flags

Personal: **MC:** gavel
Men: moustaches

Scene 2

Set: Bright silvery saucepan

Strike: Union Jacks
French and Japanese flags

Off stage: Wood (**Millie**)
Bag (**Dr Cuss**)

Personal: **Dr Cuss:** shiny badge

Scene 3

On stage: Bar
High stool
Piano
Piano stool
Barrel
Table
2 low stools at the table
Port
Glen McCraggie
Duster

Bottles with drink

Off stage: Bag (**Miss Statchell**)
Dr Cuss's bag, dark goggles (**Griffin**)

Personal: **Miss Statchell:** pipe, matches, flask
Burdock: leather coat, flying helmet, gauntlet, goggles

SCENE 4

On stage: Rustic table. *On it:* tub with washing
Chair
Stool
Milk churn
Bucket. In it: potatoes, knife
Bicycle
Pitchfork
Bundle. *In it:* spoons
Stick

Off stage: Barrel (**Teddy**)
Cart. *In it:* small dog, box with bottles, large jar, paper (**Fearenside**)
Bag (**Miss Statchell**)

Personal: **Miss Statchell:** notebook, pen
Griffin: cigarette, hat, glasses, gloves
Burdock: natty buttonhole

SCENE 5

Strike: Rustic table
Chair

SCENE 6

On stage: Lace curtains
Main curtains
Short stool
Tall stool
2 busts in niches
Harmonium

Stool
Work table. *On it:* papers
Drawers. *In them:* books
2 candles
Cash box
Empty collection box
Lamp
Window-pane glass (broken)

Off stage: Candle (**Bunting**)

Personal: **Miss Statchell:** pipe

SCENE 7

On stage: Debris
Rustic table. *On it:* untouched food—a pie

Off stage: Broom (**Mrs Hall**)
Beer (**Jaffers**)

SCENE 8

On stage: Chair
Rustic table. *On it:* untouched food—a pie
Pump
Bicycle

Off stage: Helmet (**Jaffers**)
Broom (**Millie**)
Bicycle (**Jaffers**)
Large ledger (**Bunting**)

Personal: **Miss Statchell:** pipe
Marvel: manacles
Jaffers: notebook

SCENE 9

On stage: Broom

Off stage: Handbag (**Miss Statchell**)

Personal: **Miss Statchell:** pipe, hat

SCENE 10

On stage: Table. *On it:* bubbling equipment, knife
Papers
Broken glass
Beaker
Swivel chair
Chair
Books
Notebooks
Oil-lamp
Curtains covered with a black material
Heavy packing case

Off stage: Handcuffs (**Jaffers**)

Personal: **Griffin:** cigarette, glasses, bandages, gloves, scarf, dressing-gown, night-shirt
Jaffers: helmet, truncheon

ACT II

SCENE 1

Off stage: Log (**Follies**)

SCENE 2

Off stage: Log
Stick
Bundle. *In it:* pie (**Marvel**)

Personal: **Marvel:** handkerchief

SCENE 3

On stage: Bar
High stool
Piano

Piano stool
Barrel
Table
2 low stools at the table
Bottles with drink
Notebooks
Barrel
Duster
Miss Statchell's bag
Glasses
Milk
Straw
Doormat
Menu
String

Off stage: Tray. *On it:* cups, plates, cake, bread knife (**Millie**)
Large brown metal catering teapot (**Mrs Hall**)
Bunting's clothes (**Adye**)

Personal: **Miss Statchell:** notebook, pipe
Adye: notebook

SCENE 4

Strike: Bar
High stool
Piano
Piano stool
Barrel
Table
2 low stools at the table
Bottles with drink
Notebooks
Barrel
Duster
Miss Statchell's bag
Glasses
Milk
Straw
Doormat
Menu
String

Personal: **Miss Statchell:** pipe

SCENE 5

On stage: Drinks table. *On it:* bottles of drink, glasses, port decanter
Chair
Desk. *On it:* newspaper, papers, quill pen. *In it:* drawers
Screen

Off stage: Books (**Marvel**)
Griffin's long coat (**PC 2**)

Personal: **Griffin:** gloves, long black stocking
Adye: pistol (six shots), whistle
PC 1: handcuffs

SCENE 6

Strike: Drinks table. *On it:* bottles of drink, glasses, port decanter
Chair
Desk. *On it:* newspaper, papers, quill pen. *In it:* drawers
Screen

Off stage: Port decanter, glass (**Dr Kemp**)

Personal: **Adye:** pistol, bullets, whistle
Burdock: flying helmet

SCENE 7

On stage: Red curtain
Table. *On it:* Union Jack cover, various weapons, rounder's bat, cane carpet-beater, stick
2 Chairs
Banner sign: "Iping Village Defence Committee. Combating the Invisible Menace"

Off stage: Long scarf (**Griffin**)

Personal: **Adye:** pistol
Wicksteed: hat

Scene 8

Strike: Red curtain
Table. *On it:* Union Jack cover, various weapons, rounder's bat, cane carpet-beater, stick
2 Chairs
Banner sign: "Iping Village Defence Committee. Combating the Invisible Menace"

Off stage: Paper, big placard ("Monday!") (**Newsboy 1**)
Paper, big placard ("Tuesday!") (**Newsboy 2**)
Paper, big placard ("Wednesday!") (**Newsboy 3**)
Paper, big placard ("Thursday!") (**Newsboy 4**)
Paper, big placard ("Friday!") (**Newsboy 5**)
Paper, big placard ("Saturday!") (**Newsboy 6**)
Globe (**Griffin**)

Scene 9

On stage: Chair
Door lock and key
Bed

Off stage: Bag (**Wicksteed**)
Stick and bundle (**Marvel**)

Personal: **Wicksteed:** watch, pistol
Burdock: pistol
Adye: pistol
Dr Kemp: silver fob-watch, tie

Scene 10

Set: 2 crates. *On them:* hammer
Rustic table
Chair

Strike: Chair
Door lock and key
Bed

Off stage: Spade (**Fearenside**)

Blanket (**Millie**)
Notebooks (**Marvel**)
Box and steps
Silver cloak and hat (**Marvel**)
Ice-axe (**Bunting**)
Stick (**Marvel**)
Broom (**Mrs Hall**)
Rolling-pin (**Millie**)
Bag. *In it:* grenade (**Wicksteed**)
Bag (**Nurse**)

Personal: **Adye:** pistol
Burdock: pistol
Griffin: hat, glasses

LIGHTING PLOT

This is the full lighting plot as used at the Vaudeville Theatre. It may well have to be simplified to suit other venues. Please note that not all the effects listed here are given in the main text of the play.

Property fittings required: oil-lamps, gas wall lamps
Various interior and exterior settings

ACT I

Cue 1 From SM (Page 1)
House lights, warmers on; build bright downstage area; floats, follow spot Q1 on **Freda** *in doorway* DR

Cue 2 **Freda**: "...old red white and blue" (Page 1)
Add red, white and blue gobos on gauze

Cue 3 **Freda**: "...speaks French." (Page 2)
Check

Cue 4 **All**: "Oh four!" (Page 2)
Build for end of song, then cross follow spot to **MC**

Cue 5 **MC**: "...village of Iping." (Page 4)
Big check, maintaining some floats; build green specials from the pit up on to the gauze to create shadows

Cue 6 **MC**: "Mr Thomas Marvel!" (Page 4)
Build floats; special DL *for* **MC**; *cross follow spot to* **Marvel**

Cue 7 **MC** exits (Page 5)
Lose **MC** *special*

Cue 8 **Marvel**: "Mood, maestro, please." (Page 5)
Cross-fade to green specials only

Cue 9 **Marvel**: "…worst in living memory." (Page 5)
Build snow projectors on gauze. Check green specials

Cue 10 **Marvel**: "…by the wood shed." (Page 5)
Cross-fade adjust acting area; lose green specials; build special from door L*; maintain snow; lose follow spot*

Cue 11 **Millie** exits (Page 7)
Lose special from the door

Cue 12 **Dr Cuss** cries out (Page 7)
Black-out

Cue 13 When the scene change is complete (Page 7)
Bleed through gauze to the Pub interior

Cue 14 As the gauze flies out (Page 8)
Fill from front, fairly bright warm interior by night

Cue 15 **Millie**: "And not a stitch on him." (Page 13)
Black-out

Cue 16 When the scene change is complete (Page 13)
Build downstage area, fairly bright; some floats; working light upstage

Cue 17 **Marvel**: "…at doing sod-all ..." (Page 14)
Lose working light

Cue 18 **Marvel**: "…little village of Iping." (Page 14)
Bleed through gauze to Village Green

Cue 19 As the gauze flies out (Page 14)
Fill from front, bright day exterior

Cue 20 **Mrs Hall**: "…a good lie-down." (Page 26)
Cross-fade to downstage area. Fairly bright day, leafy gobos on gauze

Cue 21 When the scene change is complete (Page 26)
Working light upstage

Cue 22 **Marvel**: "It was a bad mistake ..." (Page 27)
Lose working light

Cue 23 **Marvel**: "...to what happens next." (Page 27)
Bleed through gauze from the Vicarage

Cue 24 When the scene change is complete (Page 28)
Fill from front. Not too bright interior by night, curtains open to night sky, oil lamp on the table

Cue 25 **Miss Statchell** exits with the candle (Page 30)
Slow check in room

Cue 26 **Bunting** turns off the oil lamp (Page 30)
Big check in the room, follow on slow build of backlight through the window

Cue 27 Main curtains close (Page 30)
Adjust front light on the curtains

Cue 28 Footsteps run away (Page 31)
Cross-fade to downstage area, maintaining sky and some dressing in the room, which also acts as working light. Fairly bright night exterior; specials from door L *and window above the door*

Cue 29 **Jaffers**: "...Bruce and the Spider, Mrs Hall." (Page 32)
Lose working light

Cue 30 **Burdock** sits at the rustic table (Page 33)
Bleed through to Village Green by night

Cue 31 As the gauze flies out for the scene change (Page 33)
Fill from front. Bright night exterior

Cue 32 **Mrs Hall**: "...what with him upstairs." (Page 34)
Snap out window special

Cue 33 **Mrs Hall**: "It's Millie!" (Page 38)
Snap on window special

Cue 34 **Marvel** runs off (Page 38)
Black-out

Cue 35 When the scene change is complete (Page 39)
Build downstage area, working light up stage. Fairly bright interior by night; window gobos on blinder and door DL, *special from door* DR

Cue 36 All bunch up behind **Jaffers** at the door (Page 40)
Focus on the group

Cue 37 **Miss Statchell**: "Now just wait out *here*." (Page 42)
Cross-fade to black-out downstage; pre-set of Griffin's Room upstage

Cue 38 As blinder flies out (Page 42)
Fill from front. Moody interior by night, oil-lamp on the floor C

Cue 39 **Griffin**: "You could share with me…" (Page 44)
Begin slow check; less special on chair

Cue 40 **Griffin** turns the swivel chair around (Page 46)
Add special on the chair

Cue 41 **Miss Statchell** blows out the lamp (Page 49)
Big check; build U/V in window

Cue 42 **Millie** runs on with the lamp (Page 51)
Begin slow check; less special on the chair, follow on with slow build

Cue 43 As papers scatter (Page 55)
Build back-light on the window

Cue 44 Music (Page 55)
Fade lights to black-out

Cue 45 As the curtain falls (Page 55)
Cross-fade to working light; warmers, house lights

ACT II

Cue 46 From SM as the curtain rises (Page 56)
House lights check; warmers out; follow spot on **MC***; build bright downstage area*

Cue 47 **Follies** enter (Page 56)
Add red, white, and blue gobos on gauze; lose follow spot on **MC**

Cue 48 **All**: "…lights go down, and then…" (Page 57)
House lights out

Cue 49 **Marvel** enters (Page 57)
Cross-fade to bright day exterior; leafy gobos on gauze; no working lights up stage

Cue 50 **Griffin**: "God help you all" (Page 60)
Black-out

Cue 51 When the scene change is complete (Page 60)
Bleed through gauze to the Pub interior

Cue 52 As the gauze rises (Page 61)
Fill from front, bright interior by day

Cue 53 **Griffin**: "Ha!" (Page 66)
Slow check-down

Cue 54 Griffin whistles (Page 68)
Adjust for **Marvel's** *entrance*

Cue 55 **Griffin**: "And now—goodbye." (Page 69)
Bleed through gauze to the Pub interior

Cue 56 **Adye**: "…he *is* invisible." (Page 71)
Cross-fade to downstage area; working light upstage; night exterior

Cue 57 **Mrs Hall**: "…having me on." (Page 72)
Lose working light

Cue 58 When the scene change is complete (Page 73)
Cross-fade to bright interior by night; curtains open to night sky; gas lamps on the wall either side of the french windows

Cue 59 **Marvel** runs out (Page 86)
Cross-fade to downstage area; working light upstage; night exterior

Cue 60 **Burdock**: "How about you, Miss Statchell?" (Page 88)
Lose working light upstage

Cue 61 **Marvel** runs off (Page 89)
Cross-fade to fairly bright interior by night; red curtains at rear; some floats

Cue 62 **Bunting**: "...breaking a few windows." (Page 89)
Check; specials or follow spots on **Bunting** *and* **Marvel**

Cue 63 **Marvel**: "...to rescue you." (Page 90)
Restore lighting as at opening of the scene

Cue 64 **Bunting**: "...are some volunteers." (Page 90)
Flicker lights and dim to a red glow

Cue 65 All the men run into the auditorium (Page 92)
Cross-fade to downstage area; lose working light upstage

Cue 66 **Adye**: "...started already." (Page 97)
Black-out

Cue 67 Smash of a crashing train and a chord (Page 97)
Build special on door DL

Cue 68 **Newsboy 1**: "Read All About It!" (Page 97)
Cross-fade to special on door DR

Cue 69 **Newsboy 2**: "Extra!" (Page 98)
Cross-fade to special on door DL; *build flame projector on gauze*

Cue 70 **Newsboy 3**: "Star News Standard!" (Page 98)
Cross-fade to special on door DR; *flame projector; build special on* **Griffin** *behind gauze*

Cue 71 **Newsboy 4**: " Late Night Final!" (Page 98)
Cross-fade to special on door DL, *flame projector, special on* **Griffin**

Cue 72 **Newsboy 5**: "Special Edition!" (Page 99)
Cross-fade to special on door DR; flame projector; *build special on* **Griffin** *behind gauze*

Cue 73 **Newsboy 6** exits (Page 99)
Build downstage area; working light upstage; fade special effects and flames

Cue 74 **Marvel**: "...to the Invisible Man." (Page 99)
Lose working light

Cue 75 Village music (Page 99)
Bleed through gauze to the Cell

Cue 76 When the scene change is complete (Page 100)
Fill from front, bright interior by day; barred window gobos

Cue 77 **Adye**: "In which case——" (Page 102)
Flare lamps to create explosion

Cue 78 **Burdock**: "He's here." (Page 107)
Black-out

Cue 79 The gauze and blinder fly in (Page 107)
Build cloud projector on gauze; working light upstage

Cue 80 **Fearenside**: "He's a-coming." (Page 108)
Lose working light; bleed through gauze to the Village Green

Cue 81 As the gauze flies out (Page 108)
Fill from front. Stormy day, maintain clouds on set

Cue 82 As the gauze and blinder fly slowly in (Page 113)
Slow cross-fade to build downstage area, maintaining dressing on tableau, which also acts as working light

Cue 83 **Marvel**: "...little two up in the air." (Page 113)
Lose working light

Cue 84 **Marvel**: "But——" (Page 114)
Bleed through gauze to finale

Cue 85 As the gauze flies out (Page 114)
Fill from front. Bright full up

Cue 86 **All**: "Ooh." (Page 115)
Build special on **Marvel** *in the auditorium box*

Cue 87 Marvel leaves box (Page 115)
Lose special

Cue 88 MD takes the call (Page 115)
Build special on him

Cue 89 MD completes the call (Page 116)
Lose his special

Cue 90 Calls completed (Page 116)
Warmers, house lights; lose stage

EFFECTS PLOT

ACT I

Cue 1 **Freda**: "Evening." (Page 3)
Deep male voice: "Evening."

Cue 2 **Marvel**: "...living memory." (Page 5)
Cold wind

Cue 3 **Marvel** indicates the pub (Page 5)
Mix in pub piano

Cue 4 **Marvel** exits into the auditorium (Page 5)
Cut wind and pub piano

Cue 5 **Mrs Hall**: "...I might pay attention." (Page 8)
Gust of wind and snowflakes

Cue 6 **Miss Statchell** exits (Page 9)
Gust of wind and snowflakes

Cue 7 **Burdock**: "Isn't that the truth?" (Page 11)
Loud gust of wind and snowflakes

Cue 8 **Miss Statchell**: "Now if I could just——" (Page 18)
Yapping of a dog

Cue 9 **Griffin**: "How dare you!" (Page 20)
Growl of a dog

Cue 10 To open Scene 5 (Page 26)
Bird-song

Cue 11 **Wicksteed** exits (Page 27)
Fade out bird-song

Cue 12 After the musical drone (Page 30)
Tapping at the window followed by the pane being smashed

Cue 13 All run to the window (Page 31)
Running feet on gravel

Cue 14 As **Mrs Hall** steps out of the wood shed (Page 32)
Pub piano, off: "Bird in a Gilded Cage" (or from pit)

Cue 15 **Jaffers**: " ... what other explanation is there?" (Page 33)
Crash of glass

Cue 16 **Griffin** (*off*): "I want to be left alone!" (Page 34)
Crash

Cue 17 **Miss Satchell** enters, UL (Page 35)
Pub piano, off: "Just a Song at Twilight" (or from pit)

Cue 18 **Miss Statchell**: "…made of wood, you know." (Page 36)
Scream and breaking of a window

Cue 19 All react to a musical sting (Page 36)
Ring of a bicycle bell

Cue 20 Bicycle rides off UL (Page 37)
Loud crashing and rolling of dustbins

Cue 21 **Miss Statchell**: "What with?" (Page 42)
Sound of a bolt; then door closes

Cue 22 To open Scene 10 (Page 42)
Bubbling

Cue 23 **Griffin**: "…call my problem 'disfigurement'." (Page 43)
Cheat out bubbling

Cue 24 All crash in (Page 45)
Restore bubbling

Cue 25 **Griffin** turns around in the chair (Page 46)
Cheat out bubbling

Cue 26 **Jaffers** aims another blow (Page 54)
Clonk

Cue 27 Curtains flap (Page 55)
Big smash of breaking glass

ACT II

Cue 28 To open Scene 2 (Page 57)
Bird-song

Cue 29 **Griffin**: "Yes." (Page 59)
Sound of movement

Cue 30 Black-out (Page 60)
Cut bird-song

Cue 31 To open Scene 3 (Page 61)
Sound of a crowd

Cue 32 To open Scene 4 (Page 71)
Bells ring out an alarm

Cue 33 Scene-change music (Page 73)
Cut bells

Cue 34 **Marvel**: "…at school was truancy." (Page 77)
A sound

Cue 35 **Marvel**: "…the bloke ain't stable." (Page 85)
Shouts and whistles

Cue 36 To open Scene 6 (Page 86)
Owl hoots

Cue 37 **Marvel**: "…what *can* you rely on?" (Page 87)
Breaking window and scream

Cue 38 To open Scene 7 (Page 89)
Hubbub in auditorium at low level

Cue 39 **Bunting**: "…are some volunteers." (Page 90)
Cut hubbub

Cue 40 **Marvel**: "…and a Jersey cow." (Page 94)
Cow's moo

Cue 41 **Griffin**: " ... Ruler of the World! (Page 96)
Bang of auditorium door

Cue 42 **Marvel**: "…interesting week." (Page 97)
Explosion

Cue 43 Black-out (Page 97)
Whistle of approaching train, and big smash, then montage of mayhem

Cue 44 **Newsboy 6** exits (Page 99)
Fade out montage

Cue 45 After a brief pause (Page 102)
Church clock starts to strike twelve

Cue 46 **Burdock**: "Interfered with his tap-dancing." (Page 102)
Last chime of church clock

Cue 47 **Adye**: "In which case——" (Page 102)
Huge explosion

Cue 48 **Adye**: "What the hell's going on?" (Page 102)
Army-style gibberish

Cue 49 **Adye**: "*All* of them?" (Page 102)
Army-style gibberish

Cue 50 **Adye**: "I'll be out as soon as I can." (Page 102)
Army-style gibberish

Cue 51 **Marvel** exits (Page 104)
Shouted orders, revving engines, vehicles driving off

Cue 52 To open Scene 10 (Page 108)
Bells ring out an alarm

Cue 53 **Kemp** reaches centre and is still (Page 108)
Cut bells

Cue 54 **Wicksteed** rolls a grenade (Page 110)
Soft explosion and smoke